# KARL-HEINZ SCHRADT

# THE MAN FROM THE SAND

## PAGES OF THE FILM:
### THE ENGAGING NARRATIVE EDITION

**GALAH BOOKS**

# CONTENTS

# FOREWORD

I grew up in a Christian-centric environment in New Zealand, much like many in the West, with limited exposure to Buddhism. It wasn't until high school that a Japanese teacher introduced me to Zen Koans, although their profound depth eluded my teenage mind. Even though I heard about 'Dharma' in my youth, I didn't explore it further.

During my postgraduate studies in Health, I delved into philosophy, finding resonance with the works of Husserl, Heidegger, and Schopenhauer. However, I soon discovered that these philosophies drew heavily from Eastern wisdom traditions of Taoism, Hinduism, and Buddhism.

Disillusioned by the inadequacy of Western philosophy and academia in addressing mental suffering, I embarked on an extensive journey to study Buddhism, Hinduism, and Eastern philosophies. These, coupled with the most practical psychological tools, laid the foundation for my books: 'A Glimpse of the Freed Mind,' 'Becoming Unshakable,' and 'Rewrite Your Narrative.' Even my fiction works, like 'The Legend of Spacecat Bob,' echo themes from Stoicism and Buddhism.

'The Man from the Sand' emerged from my contemplation on the quest to tame the mind and its transformative power. Over a decade in the making, this film, from animation to the musical score, was entirely crafted by me amidst numerous other consecutive Galah Book Titles I wrote.

Similar to narratives like the Buddha's journey, the Bhagavad Gita, or indeed, movies like "Groundhog Day," "The Neverending Story," and "The Matrix"; "The Man from the Sand" story centres on uncovering one's authentic self in a coarse materialistic world. It reflects the challenge of how our minds are often filled with detrimental cognitive detritus that focuses on physical wants, hindering the pursuit of a tranquil state.

May this story entertain and enlighten, inviting all to explore the journey of discovering an authentic self amid the chaos of existence.

Karl-Heinz Schradt
San Carlos, Mexico, December 31st, 2023.

# THE MAN FROM THE SAND

A Story
by
Karl-Heinz Schradt

"And on the pedestal, these words appear:
My name is Ozymandias, King of Kings;
Look on my Works, ye Mighty, and despair!
Nothing besides remains. Round the decay
Of that colossal Wreck, boundless and bare
The lone and level sands stretch far away."

- 'Ozymandias' by Shelley

# ACT I

# 'INTO THE VOID'

Ash had been out that night, engaging in his usual deceitful dealings. He was at The King's Arms Bar when he almost got caught in a trade that was about to go disastrously wrong. A client had taken a hit of his product in the bar and fallen to the floor, convulsing. When her partner saw what had happened, he turned to Ash and yelled, "You! You did this!"

Ash quickly fled the bar and ran onto the road without looking. A car screeched as it collided with him, and he fell to the tarmac with a thud. Within minutes, he was surrounded by flashing police and ambulance lights and the clamour of people talking and lifting him into an ambulance. He was unconscious and only vaguely aware of his situation.

Sometime later, he sensed the touch of bed sheets, the sound of equipment beeping, and the presence of hospital equipment. He was drifting further into unconsciousness, his mental activities slowing.

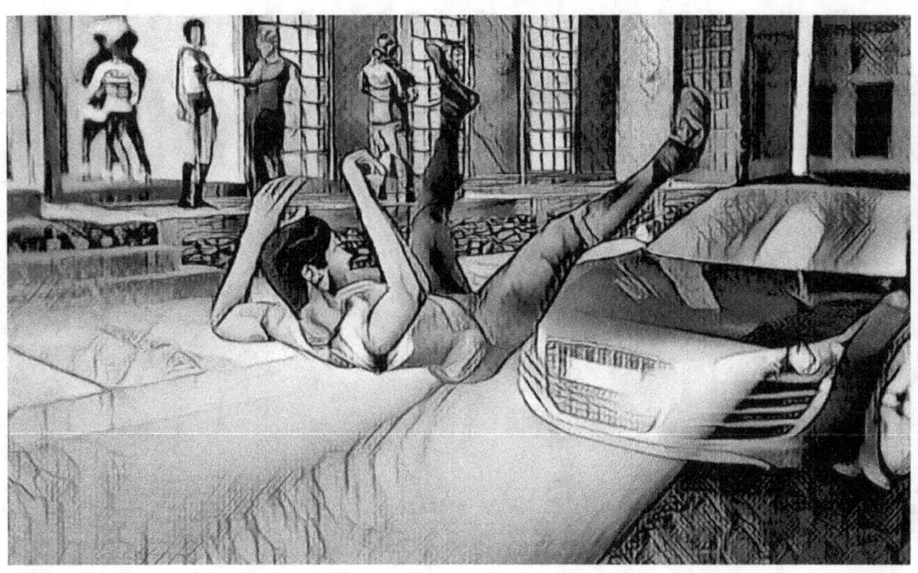

"What are we doing here?" asked Leone as he and Delvine walked through the hospital ward towards Ash's room.

"You know he has no one else," Delvine answered.

"Because he's selfish. He's burnt his bridges. It's not for us to pick up the pieces." Said Leone.

"Leone, you can stay out here if you don't want to come in. I understand. You can go home if you want," Delvine said.

"I'm not leaving you. I'll go in," he sighed.

Delvine smiled, knowing she could count on him; he was stoic on the outside but had a heart of gold.

The room was cold and quiet, except for the hum and bleep of the machines. Ash lay in the bed, looking corpse-like. The nurse had told them he was breathing independently, so there was no machine for that, and it almost looked as if he was peacefully sleeping. But Delvine knew he wasn't peaceful; he was a trickster and a cheat.

"Can he hear us?" Leone asked.
"The nurse said people sometimes can hear sounds. He'll be in this coma until the swelling in his brain has gone down, and the scans are clear." Delvine told him.
Leone looked at the still form, helpless in the bed.
"He's a fool, but no one deserves this," he said.
Delvine reached out to touch Ash.
"Ash, can you hear us?" she asked.
There was no response.

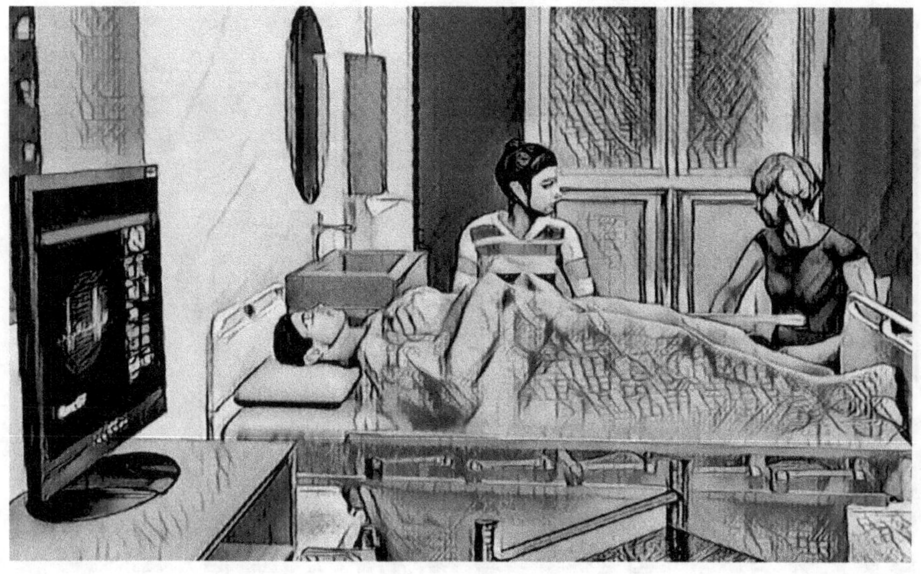

On the night shift at the city hospital, the corridors were dark, lit only by the light from the nurse's station. Ash's room was still, with the glow of machines and the occasional reflection off the vinyl tiles. On the wall was a calendar displaying the date, November 5th.

"I can't move. Can anyone hear me? Hello? I can't move," Ash's mind stirred in his damaged head.

He heard an ethereal voice. "He cannot exist in the external world anymore. There is too much damage," it spoke.

"Who said that? Who's there?" Ash answered.

There was a silence before the voice replied, somewhat surprised. "You can hear me?" it said.

"Yes! Yes, I can hear you! Who are you?" Ash called inside his mind.
"I am sorry, but there is no time to explain that now," the voice answered apologetically. "Soon, you will leave this conscious mind behind and be put back into your unconscious mind."

Ash was baffled. "What do you mean? I don't understand," he exclaimed.
"Listen to me," the voice said firmly. "Soon, you will travel back from this world through and into the Void, the ground of your unconscious mind. And from there, you will be reborn. You will remember nothing of the world that came before – you'll remember nothing of Ash."

Ash thought this was his end - undoubtedly his death, and he panicked.
"Am I dead?" he stammered.
"No. No, you're not dead. Not yet," the voice said as if it was trying to be reassuring.
The room suddenly shook and began to crumble. The world around Ash was disintegrating. The vinyl floor had changed into grey sand, and Ash and his bed rapidly sank into it. "It's happening. I'll see you on the other side," the voice came again, speaking mundanely as the world around Ash was swallowed.

Everything had become nothing. Ash was no more, like the nothingness of deep sleep. But then, like a movie projector lighting up the dark, images and scenes appeared.

"This universe is made of gateways. Portals to different realms," the voice spoke.

Firstly, he saw a seedling as it reversed back into its seed, its materials returning to the soil. Then, he was drifting through the corridors of a stone church and the entrances, which suddenly seemed to have the gravity of being gateways between distant realms in time and space.

He saw the Earth floating in the depths of space, and its circular shape became like that of a giant iris and pupil, a vast human eye.

"What you know as the world is one of many," the voice said.

He travelled into the eye and down into its nerves, the human brain, and the branches of axons. There, the tangle of neurons looked like the farthest reaches of space, like distant galaxies attached by faint and wispy links.

"You are returning to the world of your mind," the voice said.

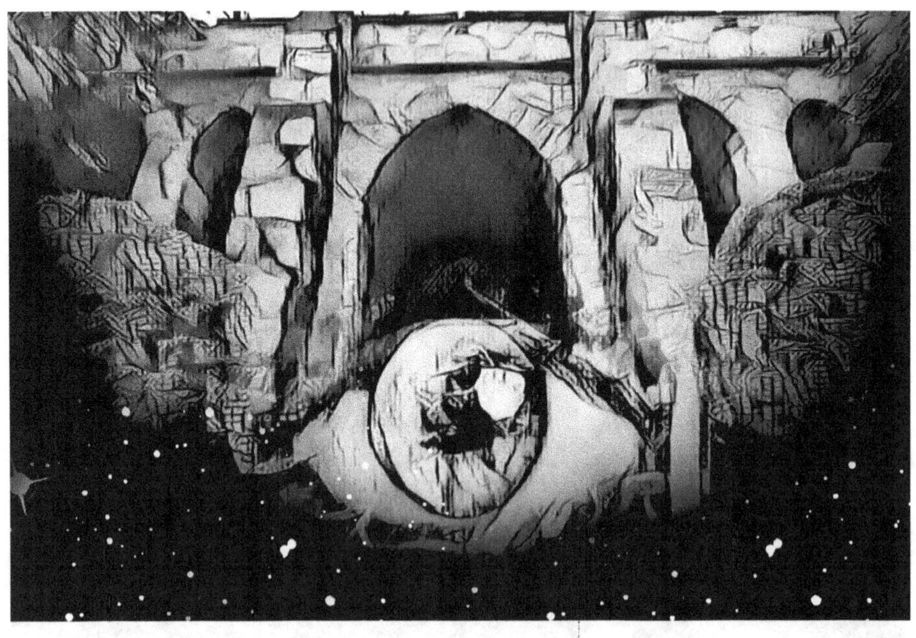

The sky above began to spin, and a black hole opened in the middle of the glittering spectacle. Then, a cloud of sand appeared from the black hole and started gathering in space.

"Just as life formed from nothing but energy – so you form," the voice said.

The sand clouded together in space as the voice continued:

"You are returning into unconsciousness - the ground of your mind. First, you remember nothing. Not even what you are. Awareness comes first… old mental habits attract attention, awareness gets focalised," the voice said.

There was a flash of light and energy amongst the sand.

"Then a consciousness is born," the voice declared.

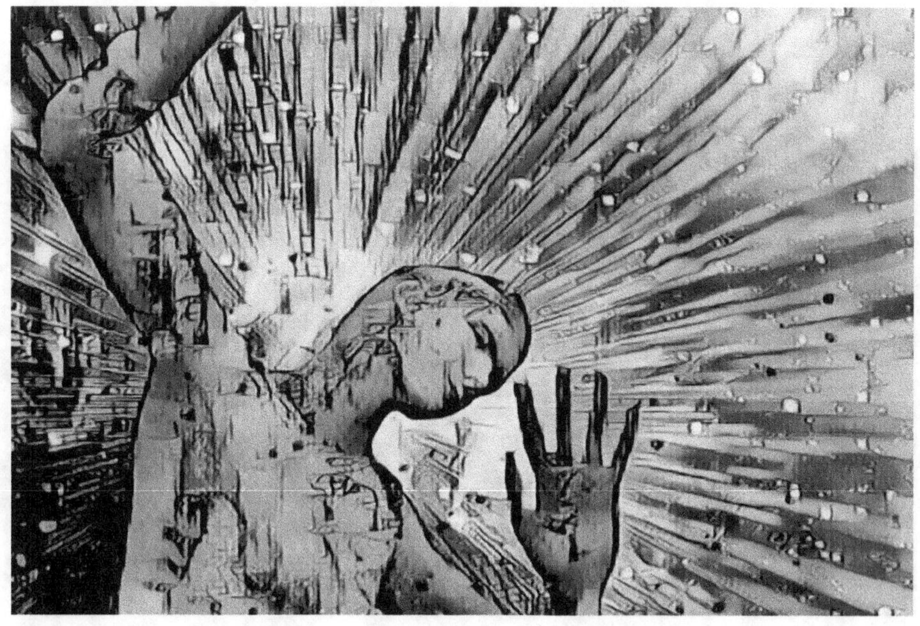

The Sand gathered rapidly into a dense cloud of shapes, and a torso, head, and limbs appeared among them.

"… and a person appears! You are reborn." the voice remarked.

By now, Sand was reborn in a complete human body and struggled among the sand, looking for air. He found an opening above him and climbed into the void, morphing from a sandy shape into organic tissues and flesh – a human being.

"Finally, you enter the world." The voice declared.

The new person found himself in a cave, still forming around him. On a flat rock sat a stone statue of a strange, mystical deity or divine entity. High above the figure, he saw a black hole in the sky. The new person looked around and at his body, confused.

"What is this?" he asked.
He remembered the sand: "I was in space. I couldn't see or hear anything; I couldn't breathe. Then I pulled myself out into here." He stammered.
He heard his voice and was surprised. "How is it that I am talking? How is it that I know anything?"

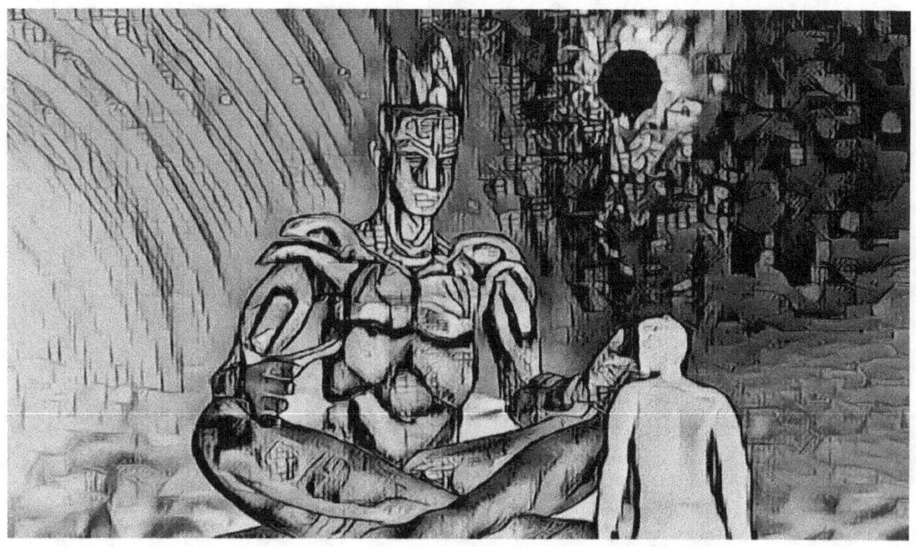

Next, he looked at the statue, realising it was the source of the voice he had been hearing. "What are you?" he asked finally.

"So, you can see me," the statue said. "I am the creator of this world, which is the origin of your mind. I am the ground of its being, but I am unimportant. I have created this world, and now it is your world to do with as you will."

The new person looked at the statue, processing the situation. "How is it that I can understand you? How is it that I know what I am? And yet, I remember so little about myself. Do I have a name?" he said, almost talking to himself.

He looked at the talking statue. "Do you have a name?"

The statue didn't speak, as it had no answer. "I feel like you don't have a name – and that doesn't matter. So, I can think of you as 'Nameless,'" he spoke.

"It is true – I have no name," Nameless confirmed.

The man standing on the sandy ground asked himself a question.

"But what am I?" he asked as he gazed at the sand beneath his feet. "All I know is that I came from this, from the sand."

"That is true," Nameless replied.

"Then I shall be known as 'Sand,'" the man declared.

"It is as good a name as any," the statue said.

Sand, intrigued, continued speaking. "I want to understand. Where am I, and what or who are you?"

"I can tell you what I am," the statue said, seeming entertained by the opportunity to share its story. "I am a part of the truth that most humans do not and will never see."

As the statue spoke, visions of different worlds and places filled Sand's mind. The figure seemed divine, filling Sand's mind with sensations and images. Sand listened attentively as ideas about the furthest reaches of space formed in his mind.

"Allow me to tell you a little about what I am," the statue said. "The nature of everything, the universe, space, and time, is more complex than you can know or imagine."

As Nameless spoke these words, landscapes under the stars appeared in Sand's mind.

"It is all a process of change, coming and going - creation, maintenance, and destruction. There are forces that you and I cannot see or measure, complex relationships between elements, and a delicate balance between forces that push and pull against each other." Nameless continued.

A vision of a circular gateway with wooden doors appeared in the middle of one of the landscapes. The doors swung open, revealing a vast night sky. The Earth appeared in the circular gateway. Sand began to understand the significance of the circle's unique properties in how the universe cycled. As the Earth hovered in the gateway, Nameless said:

"In some ways, this world is like a pocket floating alone in the vastness of space."

The Earth transformed into a sun, with people and a sky beneath it.

"Humans, come from and exist in this world," Nameless said, referring to the sentient beings of this universe. The sun's circle became that of a clock, and its arms spun rapidly countless times.

"But our world, like the universe, was born from nothing in a big bang..." Nameless said as a vision of the massive explosion of creation appeared in Sand's mind. The blast turned into a cloud of dust that clumped into sand, rocks, planets, stars, and eventually galaxies. One of the spinning galaxies transformed into a flower; Sand realised it represented the explosion of life on Earth.

"And our Earth, our universe is like an island in an ocean." Sand then saw the flower growing from an island in a vast ocean.

The following vision was of the ocean's depths, and Sand was overwhelmed by the vast amount of water. A deep underwater current swept him into a tunnel, emptying into a fountain. The head of the fountain was flower-shaped, with a stamen and petals. The fountain's centre opened with a single hole from where the water rushed out and split into several petal-like channels.

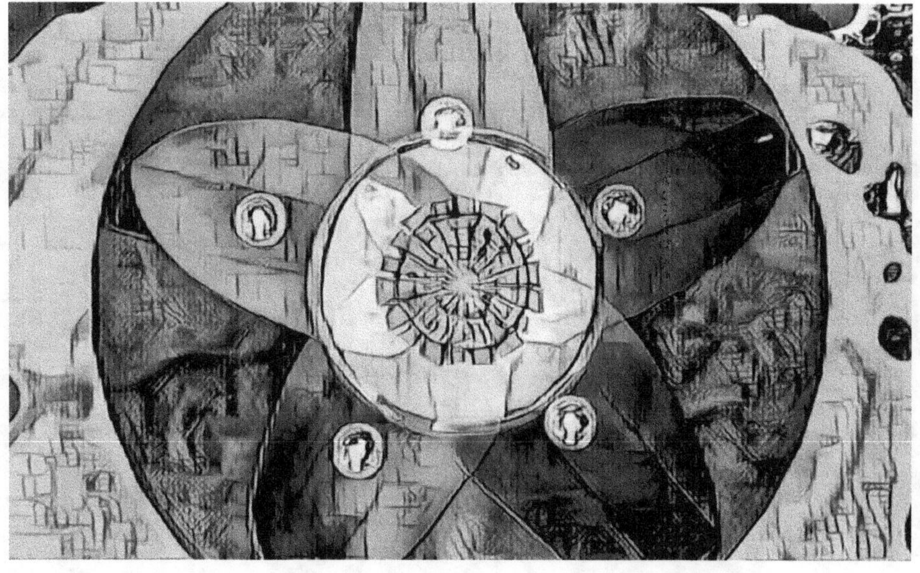

The water flowed in different directions, spilling into many rolling balls. Each ball rolled and transformed into planets moving into the depths of space.

"All worlds are born, all worlds, all universes are like petals that come from the centre of a flower. And this world that you exist in..." Sand saw that one of the balls was Earth. "...and others all come from their big bangs, their creation points. These cycles, these circles, are points of creation. These are the gates that worlds are born from." Nameless said.

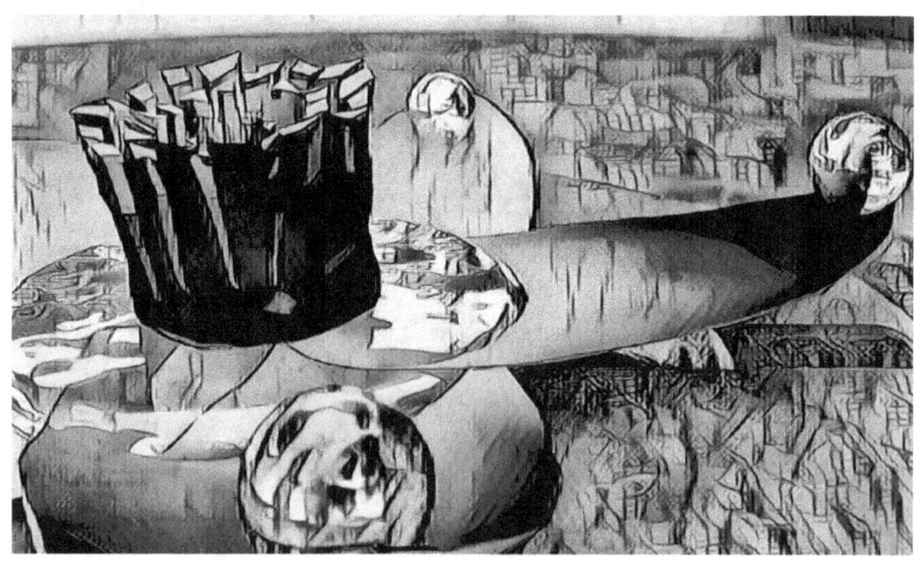

Again, Earth faded into the shape of a human eye. "And our minds are also worlds," Nameless said.

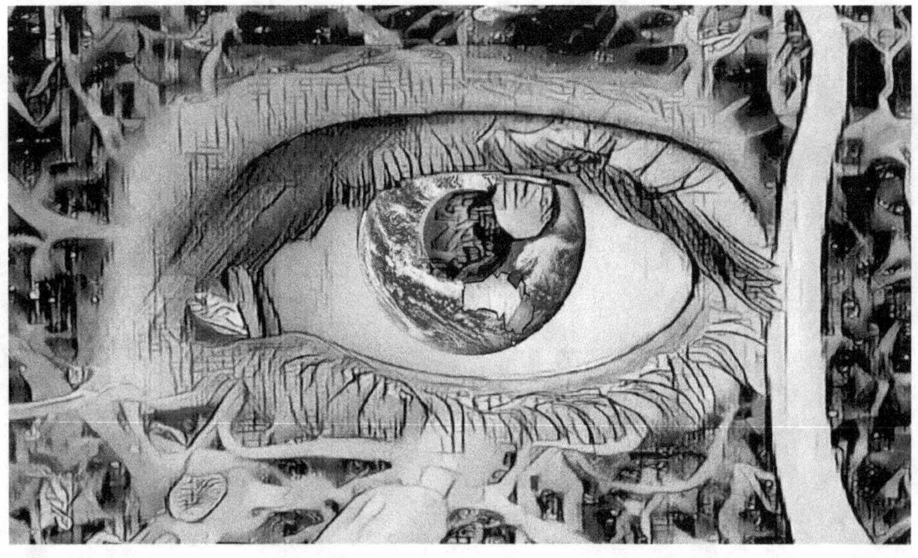

The visions faded, and Sand was back in the cave with Nameless. "I am but one of many manifestations of that great creative force from out of the void. I am not what some creatures might want to call a god. I am just a new thing. The ground of being that this world has come from the natural result of creating a new complex system. And now the rest is up to you." He said.

Sand then noticed a beam of light flooding the cave from an entrance behind him. He turned, driven by curiosity, to see what was beyond. He reached the opening, and a vast landscape lay ahead of him. He could see vast meadows, distant mountains, and dense green vegetation.

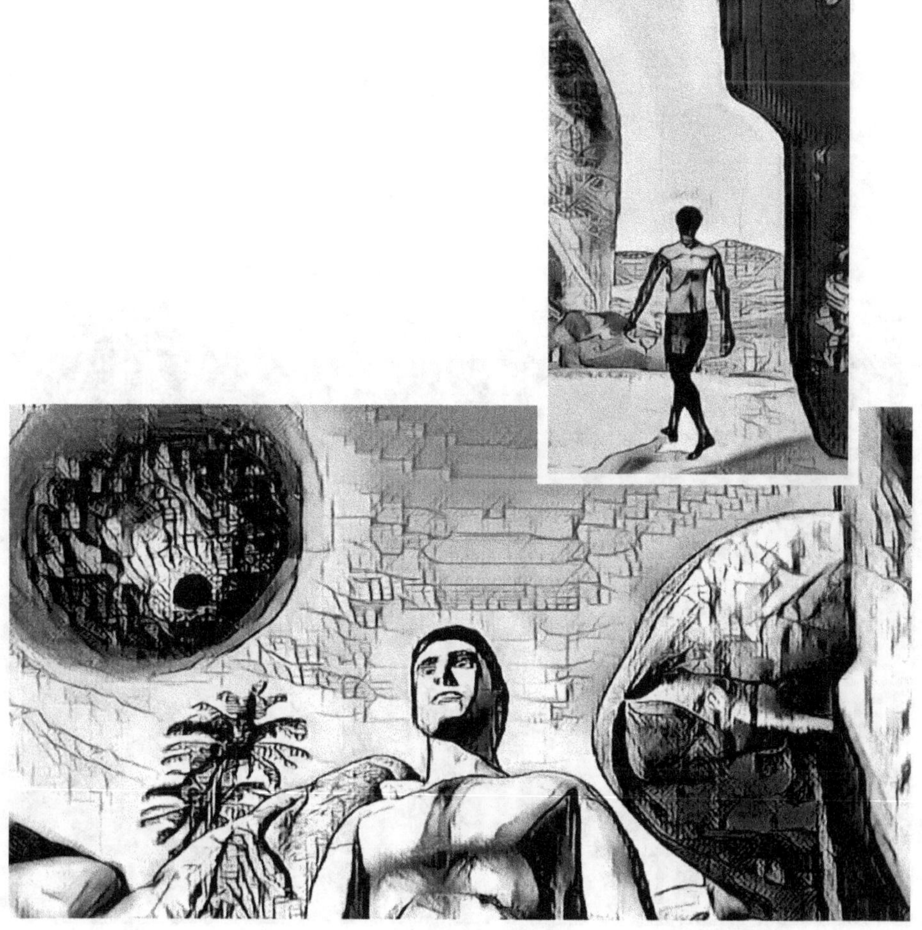

As the weeks passed, Sand enjoyed the world that Nameless had created. One night, he realised what Nameless meant when he said he was now maintaining this world. Sand had been looking at the sky and saw the black hole, constantly spinning slowly above. As he looked at it, he remembered the visions with Nameless on that first day: the creation of those worlds and all the life of the people in mysterious cities. As he looked, he found that ideas would come to him, flashes of inspiration, visions of possibilities. If he thought hard enough, he could do something extraordinary; a rain of sand would fall from the black hole and onto his world, and whatever he saw would manifest at that moment.

Over the weeks, he reached into the black hole and explored what lay inside. That void was somehow part of his subconscious or that part of his mind that he shared with it. He could manifest ideas, things, and places. He made the deep seas around him brimming with fish, trees in the forests, exciting animals, exotic birds, tigers, lakes, and waterfalls.

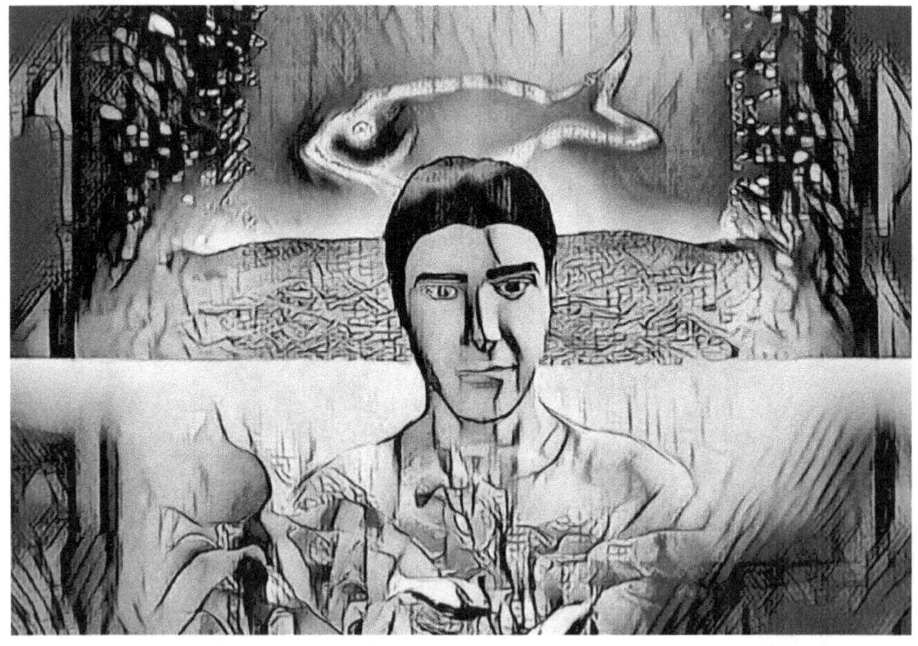

Sand wandered his new world, loving the wonder of this place. He would visit the cave from time to time and tell Nameless about his discoveries. Nameless seemed aware of, but emotionally detached from, these things from the void. He seemed more interested in Sand and his welfare. After a while, new concepts and ideas came to Sand from the nothingness. Unlike natural objects, these objects were of a human mind. It started with tables, chairs, and tools.

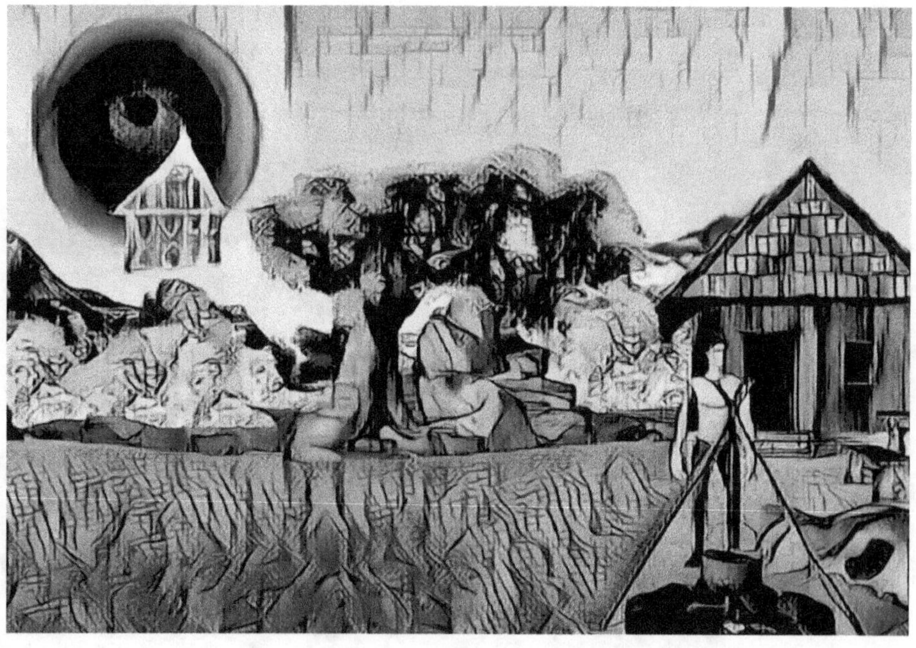

From these ideas, Sand made himself a wooden cabin in the hills, made a fireplace, and kept chickens and other animals. Each week, he remembered more: boats, canoes, and even ways to ride the wild horses. In time, he had a favourite horse, a white mare called "Mist", and a small white chicken called "Peck". Even the sea offered the friendship of a grey dolphin.

Sand didn't see Nameless for long periods as he wandered and travelled through his new world. He would return to Nameless occasionally to share his excitement and happiness. But over time, Sand's excitement seemed to wane. Nameless was an old soul who knew this situation; Sand was becoming fixated on pleasures, longing for more and more, always seeking new ways of entertainment. He sought new pleasing objects, foods, stranger sights, and sounds.

Sand visualised grand architecture, palaces, temples, golden shrines, great works of art, and images of deities and people of great beauty. He would draw them down into the forest and fields of his world and roam through them, struck by the beauty and mystery of their origin. Nameless listened and watched with interest as Sand drew more and more from the void. Nameless knew that in the void was more than just places and artworks; in that place lurked all the things that, over time, countless humans had experienced, created, and imagined.

One day, as Sand roamed, Nameless pondered to himself. "I am an ageless entity. I understand this world is an order derived from chaos in a fragile balance. Sand must maintain the balance, for too much chaos will destroy him and the world. But so far, Sand has only seen order and not chaos. I will need to show him what he has not seen."

The next time Sand appeared to see Nameless in the cave, Nameless told him:
"Now that you're here, I need you to see something."
"Gladly. You always have me do interesting things, Nameless." Sand nodded in agreement.
"Ride your white horse over the grasslands and down into the burnt valley. Leave your horse behind and keep walking down into the valley's depths. At the bottom, I want you to meet the destructor."
"The destructor?" Sand said, wide-eyed.
"Yes, I created, you maintain, and he destroys," Nameless told him.

And so, Sand took his horse and rode the distance across the grassland and into the burnt valley. The burnt valley was grassless; the rocks were rusty orange and radiated heat from being baked in the sun. The trees were dried up and knotted, all having died long ago. The place was without water, whipped with dry winds and dust. Seeing the end of the valley, a dead end of rocky crags, Sand tied up Mist and walked further on foot.

He apprehensively wandered into the cavern, treading quietly. His eyes searched along the rocky walls until he saw a slope of sand that reached up the cliff wall towards an old doorway, the remnant of an ancient temple cut into the cliff rock. In the empty opening, the inside of the temple was dark and black, and he saw nothing inside.

Sand heard a sound behind him as he tried to see into the darkness. Surprised, he ducked behind a rock and cautiously looked over it. He saw a water buffalo he had transported from the black hole into this world weeks ago stumbling into the canyon. He could see that the beast was sick and could barely walk. It soon fell, gasping onto the sand of the canyon floor. He no sooner had the beast fallen than something stirred in the darkness of the archway. Two white eyes appeared, staring at the beast. The eyes moved to the entrance, and a black figure dressed in a black cloak emerged from the doorway and moved to the dying beast. Sand stayed low and out of sight, knowing without hesitation that this was the destructor.

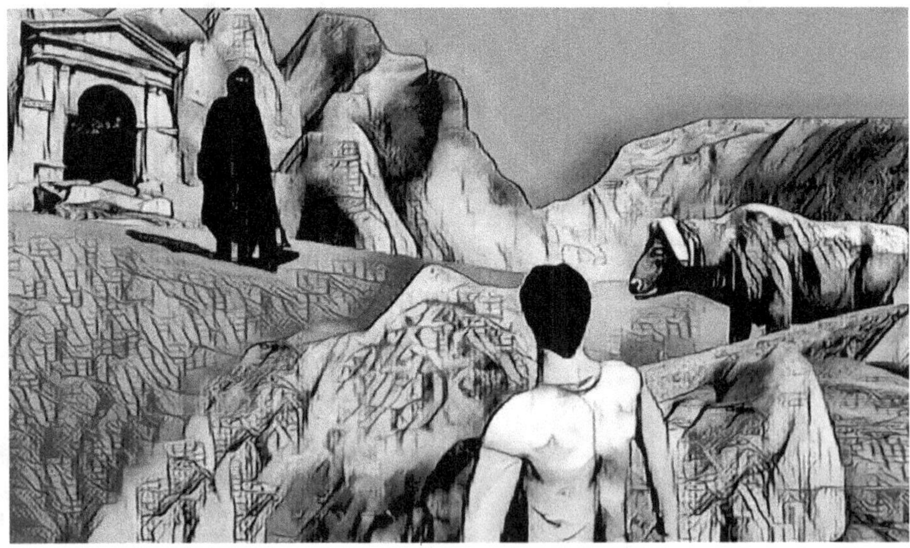

The phantom-like figure knelt at the head of the water buffalo. The beast did not resist the figure's ominous presence. Instead, it seemed resigned that it was time to die and went limp against the hot sand. The phantom held a black hand above its snout, and particles started to come from the creature's body. A steady stream of sand poured out, drawn by the destructor, before the sand ascended into the black hole above. As this happened, the water buffalo's body was stripped of its tissues until only its bones remained. Once the phantom had done this, it returned to the darkness of the temple entrance.

Back in Nameless's cave, the skies rumbled with thunder as a storm rolled in that evening. Sand had just taken a seat before his mentor, the wise statue.

"I saw what you sent me to see. I don't know how to explain it. The destructor absorbed that creature. It just disappeared into bones." Sand said. "All things are transient. They come into this world, abide for a time, and then cease." Nameless told him. "You, Sand, are half me, a creator, and half him, a destroyer. This world is your responsibility. Do not lose control of what you extract from the void. When you take from there, you are changing this world in a way you may not be able to control."

"So, what do I do?" Sand asked.
"Try to be happy with what you have," Nameless answered. "I shall teach you to notice when strong feelings are in your mind, and the practice called meditation. You will tame racing thoughts by sitting, letting your thoughts, breathing, and feelings settle, and noticing the sounds of birds and insects."

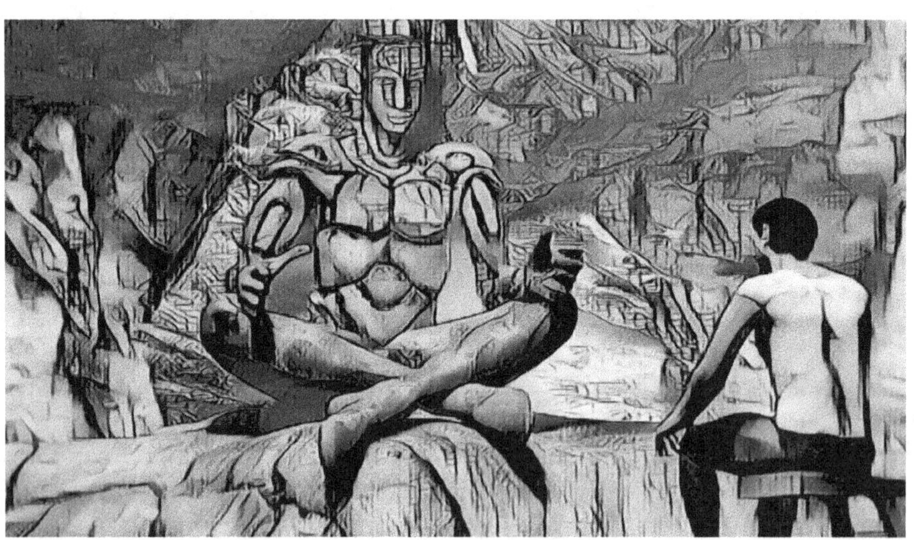

After some weeks of practice, in which Sand learned to calm himself, Nameless realised that Sand had learned the importance of self-discipline and strength. He occasionally searched the void for new pleasures and discoveries but tried not to get caught up. However, Sand tried to live grateful for the land, trees, animals, simple cottages, and lifestyle. When his thoughts strayed, he would visit Nameless to straighten them out. The weeks passed, and Sand enjoyed his pastimes. He would meet with his dolphin friend and ride his favourite horse, Mist.

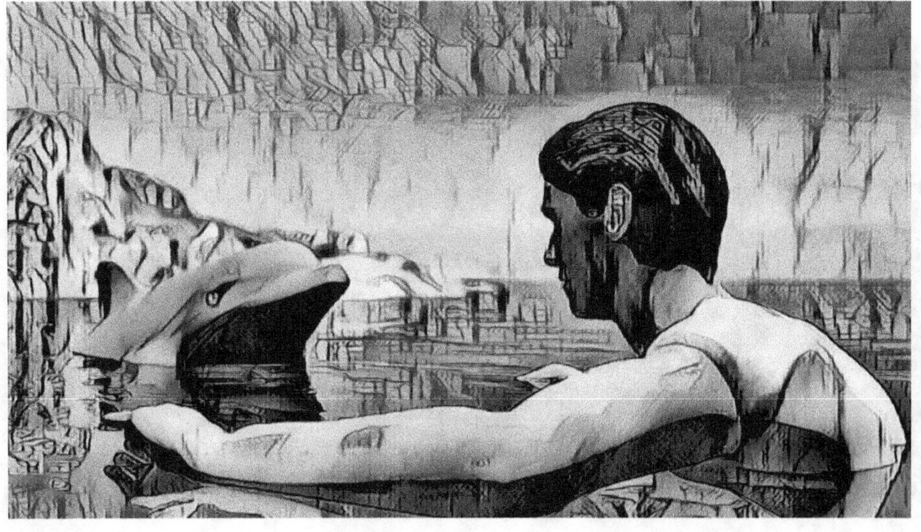

But one day, things took an unexpected turn. Sand had ridden Mist along their favourite track, the grasslands, along the beach, and they had settled into a trot in the beautiful, lush forest on the way back to the cabin. Suddenly, with a roar from the thick ferns and bushes, a tiger in brilliant orange, white, and black stripes leapt out. Sand ordered the panicked Mist into a gallop, but the tiger jumped and hooked its mighty claws into Mist's hindquarters, dragging the poor horse to the ground and sending Sand tumbling off.

Sand, though winded, tried to get up but needed a moment to overcome his shock. In the meantime, he heard the roars of the fearsome wild beast and the whinnies of Mist. By the time he had oriented himself, the tiger had gone, and Mist was covered in blood and cuts and barely moving. The attack had left Mist at death's door.

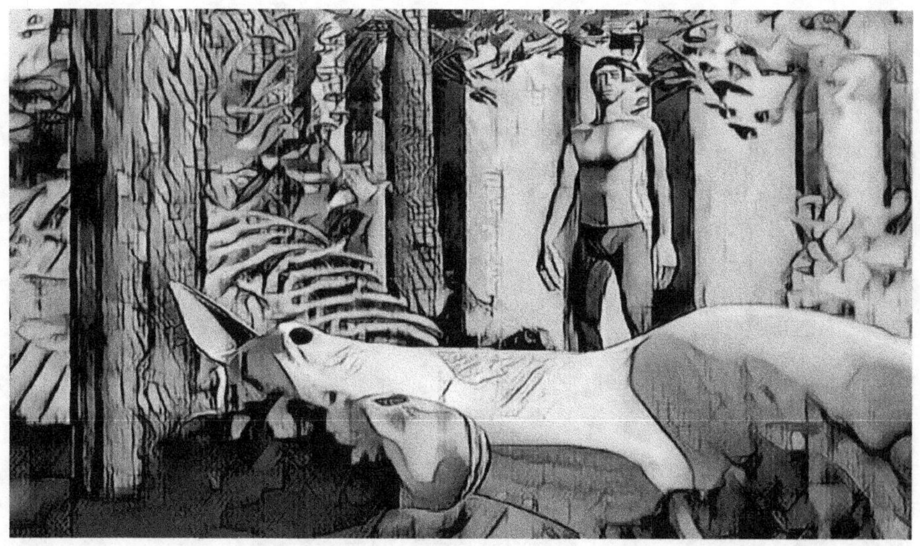

Sand brought a horse-drawn cart to Mist, and after loading Mist onto it, he returned her to the farm. He cared for her through the night, dressing and cleaning her wounds. But when the Reaper appeared on the hill above his cabin, he knew the situation was hopeless and that it would only be a matter of time before Mist succumbed.

The next day, he went to Nameless, seeking his help.
"Can't we stop the Reaper?" he asked him.
"I, and we, cannot. This world exists because another ends. Without destruction, there is no creation. You must accept with nobility - that this world, and the entities in it, are a temporary gift."

Sand shook with anger.
"It's crazy! I don't have to accept anything!" he muttered.
Nameless allowed a moment to pass as Sand processed his feelings. Sand, meanwhile, struggled to align his denial with his desire to trust and believe in Nameless's words.
Nameless spoke gently:
"And yet, you will have grown up if you accept this. Regain your tranquillity. Let your friend go and treasure what you still have." He advised.

Sand stood, avoided looking at the statue and said:
"Sometimes, Nameless, I think you ask the impossible."
Sand walked towards the exit of the cave, but before he left, Nameless told him:
"There are forces beyond you, Sand."
Sand stopped to listen.

"Look at the void. You don't control it. You only control yourself. Run a clean world. Be just and reasonable. Avoid the wrong and the unbeneficial. Make life in harmony with the world. Respect your place and this world and the power of the void. Embrace forgiveness, gratitude, and understanding." Nameless finished.

Sand stood thinking for a moment, and then, without a word, he walked out into the dark, rainy night.

Two days later, Sand returned to the cave, his face etched with sleepless nights and overthinking. He sat before Nameless and declared:
"I've come to say goodbye."
"You're leaving?" Nameless said without surprise.
"It's cool now. The horses must go to the grasslands to graze." Sand declared, trying to cover up his inner turmoil with excuses.
"I see. But I sense you still hate the reaper." Nameless told him.
"With all my heart." Sand said. "I'll see you when I return, Nameless."
"Safe travels, Sand." Said Nameless.
And Sand was gone.

Sand stood lost in thought, looking at the waves crashing on his favourite beach in the moonlight. He longed for a world with no death, danger, or illness. Nameless's advice to control his desires and limit his wants only confused and annoyed him. He needed to clear his head, so he turned to the black hole in the sky.
"What's still in you?" he asked it. Then he sighed. "I wish you'd just disappear."

Nameless, who mainly meditated, thought about Sand. Sand's situation concerned him. He could sense the hatred in Sand's heart because Sand hadn't accepted the world and their roles in it, including the Reapers.

Sand travelled through his world and discovered new places. He and the horses found grasslands, mountain pastures, and secluded creeks, rivers, and lakes. But Sand was unhappy. At night, he thought about old pleasures, Mist, significant buildings, and incredible inventions that could fly and travel fast. He saw visions of the tiger and the Reaper and felt a strange call from the black hole. He tossed and turned, thinking about death and his own identity.

The question of his identity became more prominent in his mind. He thought that Nameless, if he were there, would tell him to let go of such thoughts, but he didn't.

Soon, he dreamed of a mysterious door by a rock face in a forest. In his sleep, he entered the door and walked through the catacombs to a great hall with statues and carvings. A large table was there, and two figures stood out: a wise man and a warrior with swords. Behind the table was a marble frieze with a circular design of a pig trying to eat a chicken, which attempted to eat a snake, which circled back to the pig.

He looked around the room. Suddenly, three visions of himself walked in from different corners and sat at the table. A meal appeared, and they ate hungrily.

But arguments broke out over the food, and they stood yelling at each other. Their heads turned into a chicken, a pig, and a snake, like the picture on the wall. Sand woke up at that point in the dream.

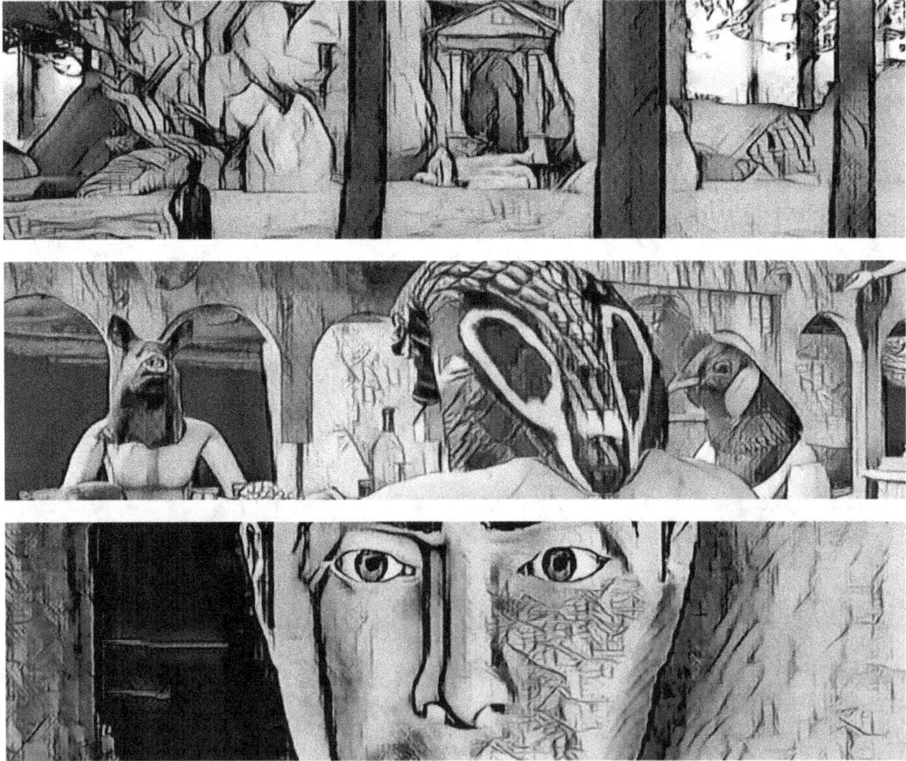

Despite his troubled mind, he continued his journeys in unknown parts of his world. One day, he and the horses stopped by a mountain lake to rest. As he gathered water, he thought about his reflection in the water. His reflection spoke to him.

"There's power in the void. I've seen it!" it declared.

Sand gasped. His reflection smiled.

"Don't you want to know what I know?" it asked.

Suddenly, to Sand's great surprise, his reflection leaned towards him and fell out of the water. Sand leapt back in shock as his doppelganger flew through the air with a yell of delight, only to fall to the ground in front of him. Somehow, this new being had come into existence in Sand's world. It sneered in satisfaction; it had achieved its desire.

"So, I made it!" it declared.

It looked at the ground under its feet, savouring the new reality. It took some of the watery soil and rubbed it between its fingers.

"It feels more interesting than I expected - this wetness, water, this soil," it cooed.

It smiled to itself. "At last, I'm real."

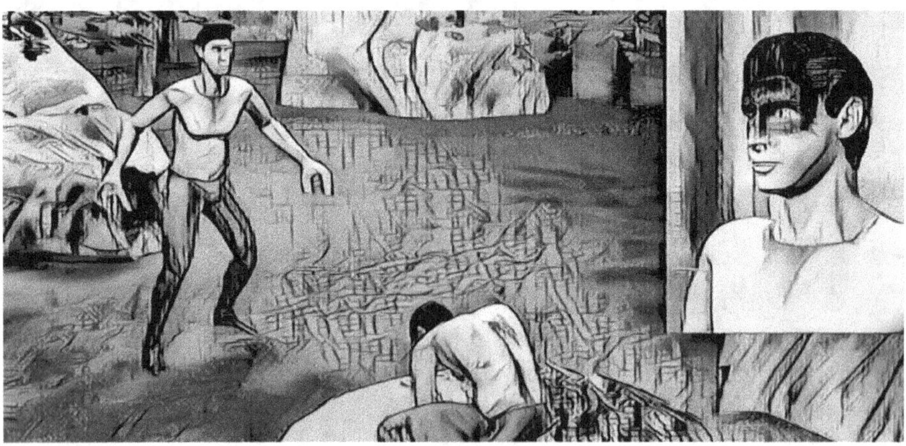

Sand, now angered by the entity's appearance, yelled, "Go away! I don't know how you've come from there!"

But his double just laughed.

"Sand. I'm a real admirer of the name. And you shall call me 'Mud'," Mud declared, rubbing mud on his face as if to define his uniqueness.

Mud looked Sand over and smiled approvingly. "So powerful! Like a god!" he said. But then his face became hostile. "You have used your will and the constant interference of that fool to keep us out of the world," Mud sneered. Sand realised 'that fool' he was talking about Nameless. "But I'm your right-hand man. You and I own this world. Control it. Let us build a kingdom - you and I." it offered.

Sand turned from him and sat on the mud in the meditation position that Nameless had taught him.

"What are you going to do? Will you be a King or a plant?" Mud sneered.

Sand took several breaths and directed his attention to the sounds of birds and insects and towards his breathing, soothing his racing thoughts. "You don't exist," he thought to himself.

After a moment, his mind had calmed. When he opened his eyes, the entity called Mud was gone.

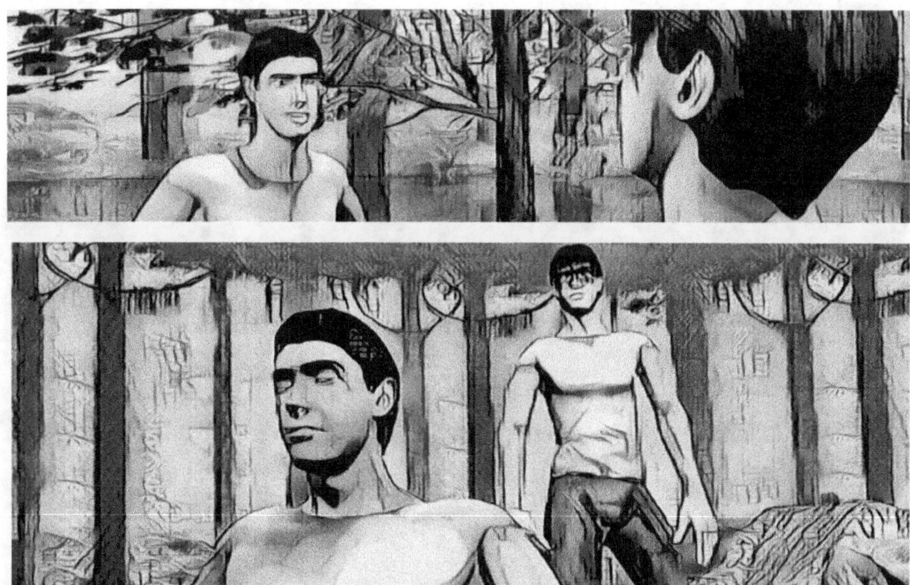

# ACT II

# 'STORMCLOUDS'

Nameless, deep in meditation, he sensed a gentle presence approaching his cave. As a small white chicken walked in, he widened his concentration on his surroundings. It was 'Peck', Sand's beloved chicken.
"Hello, my friend," Nameless said.
Nameless sensed its loneliness. Peck had come visiting, hoping to find Sand finally back from his travels.
"Maybe you worry for him," Nameless told the tiny bird. Nameless's voice saddened, knowing that Sand's thoughts had grown away from his previously simple life. "The desires of his heart take control. His mind ran wild, his farm grew with weeds, and the horses ran away. Once again, untamed. The dolphins no longer wait for him. He does not wander this world and is no longer joyful or grateful." Nameless said.

However, to the bird's delight, Sand returned to his cottage a week later. But Sand immediately sat by his small pond and was preoccupied and distant. He had not even returned to Nameless's cave to announce his arrival. He sat watching his chicken happily pecking at the grass, lost in his thoughts.

In the corner of his eye, he saw new visions: two reflections in the pond's water – a man and a woman. Somehow, they seemed familiar, as if from a latent memory.
"More? No, not again!" he declared, remembering Mud's previous terrifying appearance.

To his surprise, it was then that he heard Mud's voice:
"Honestly, you worry about nothing." He laughed.
Sand turned to see him sitting at his outside table. Mud chuckled and gestured back to the reflections in the pond.
"You can bring them into this world." He told Sand.

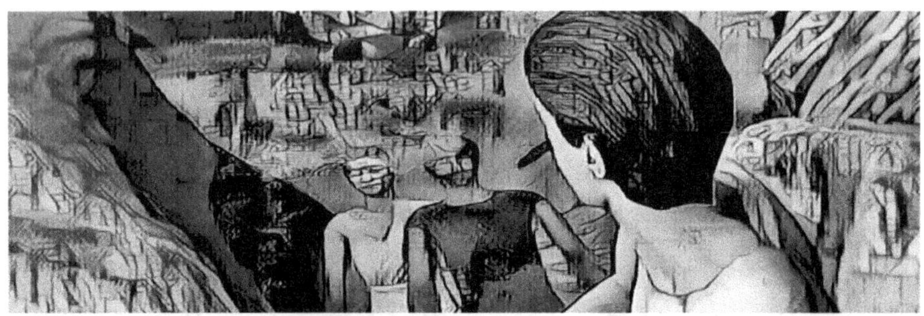

Sand gazed back at the water, and to his amazement, a female hand appeared. Although uncertain, he took the hand and helped a new entity into his world, much like Mud had appeared. It was the oddly familiar woman he had seen in the reflection. Soaked, she took her first breaths.

"I'm alive.... breathing this... air!" she exclaimed, savouring the feeling of air in her lungs.

Sand stared at her, stunned.

"I'm called... Sand." He stammered, "And you are?"

Mud chuckled in amusement from the table.

"She's called Air, of course! Isn't it obvious?" he grinned.

Sand would not know it, but she looked just like his old friend in his previous life, Delvine.

Mud stood and walked towards the fireplace, which sprang into flame as he clicked his fingers.

"Now, see how easy that was?" he said impatiently. He gestured to Sand. "Come with me and look into the fire. Your next loyal friend awaits," he said as he gazed into the flames.

Sand was entranced and intrigued, so he walked over to the fire. Amidst the flames, a person was forming.

"Meet 'Fire,'" Mud declared with a grin.

Sand hesitated but then reached out and took the fiery hand. The hand didn't burn him; he could pull the glowing man, who was made of coal and embers, from the fire. The form quickly cooled and became a flesh and blood man. Sand didn't realise it, but the man looked just like his old friend Leone from his previous life.

"These are your servants, Sand. They will help you build an empire," Mud declared.
Sand turned to Mud, disgusted by his grandiosity and autocratic demeanour.
"No empires, Mud. Having others in this world is enough for me." he told him.
"Nothing is ever enough. Not now," Mud sneered, clearly having other intentions.

Sand looked at the three figures, now fully manifested in his world. He panicked, knowing he had lost control of the situation. He thought of Nameless and knew he needed help as soon as possible.
"I need to go." he said, running away from them towards Nameless's cave.
"Go! I'll do it all for you!" Mud yelled after him.

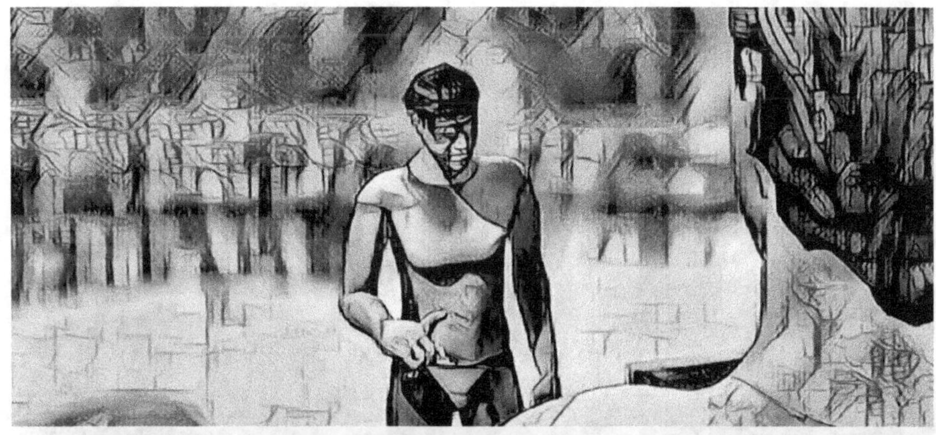

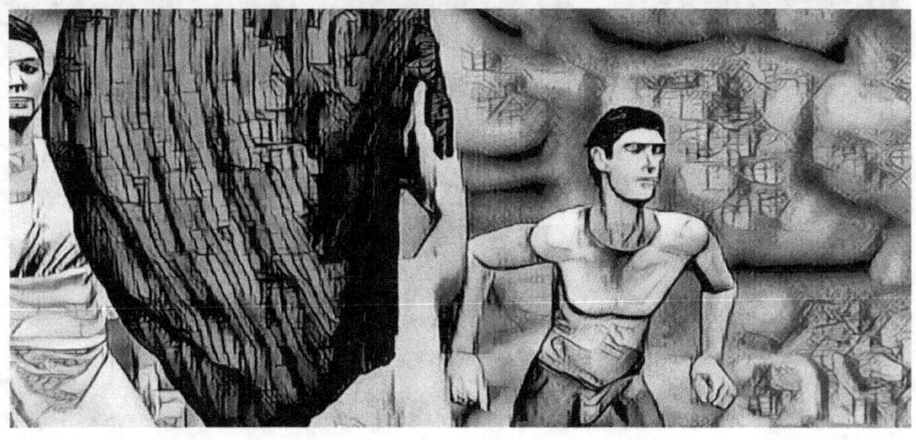

Mud turned to his new minions, Air and Fire, as Air watched Sand run away.

"He made us?" she asked, feeling responsible for her creator. However, Mud shrugged.

"More or less." he mumbled.

"Then we must help him." Fire proclaimed. Mud nodded, seeing an opportunity to influence them both.

"You will. But he lacks ambition. With your help, he can achieve greatness." he told them.

"Greatness?" Fire asked, considering Mud's words.

"What is that?" Air asked.

"Does he want these things?" Fire asked further. Mud laughed.

"Oh, Fire! Why wouldn't he?" he roared. Then, his tone became serious.

"I've been here longer than you. I've been watching since the beginning."

Mud pointed to the black hole above.

"See up there? Evil forces are in that place." he stated, trying to scare the others. "But there are good forces, too." he added. He gestured for Air and Fire to follow him.

"Come! We will help Sand become stronger." he said.

Sand ran across the grasslands as a thunderstorm rolled in. Lightning flashed, and rain poured down as he reached Nameless's cave. Sand ran in and turned around to ensure the entities hadn't followed him.

"I see him, Sand. He brings great change. He's connected to the void and finds ideas and objects within it. This creation will become his. It will be a place of pride, lust, and arrogance disguised as pleasure. I'm afraid the others are naive. They are his pawns." Nameless told him sadly.
Sand knew immediately that what Nameless said was true. He had known Mud was evil from the moment they met.
"I'm afraid he's attracting the destructor towards you." Nameless announced. "Destruction can be death or great chaos, madness, sickness, delusion, or suffering. These are all shades of the same thing." Nameless said.
"What do I do?" Sand asked.

Meanwhile, Mud had already started his work. He had created a small city on a small rocky hill with defensive structures and barracks manned by soldiers taken from the void. Air and Fire watched as Mud, smiling and laughing, created a monument to himself from the ground.

"And there will be an army of servants for me! For all of us! Slaves!" he said grandly, shaking his fist. "I will take them from the void."

Mud surveyed his creation; disapprovingly, his eyes settled on the forests. "We will burn these forests down." he sneered. "We will bring forth more animals, make them work for our causes, and then we will have no enemies to fear."

Both Air and Fire seemed uncertain about the rapid changes Mud was creating, but it was Fire who spoke first:
"These buildings, those armies. Mud, this world was calmer and more peaceful before them," he told Mud. "Return them. Put them back in the void. I'm going to find Sand and ask him what he desires." he insisted.

Mud was outraged, but he managed to calm himself. He had big plans and needed Fire to be a part of them.
"I understand your concerns, Fire," he said, feigning concern. "Come. I want to show you something that will help you understand."

Mud led Fire to the other side of the hill. There, a rocky outcrop overlooked a lava flow.

"This world is still so young, it's like an infant," Mud told Fire as they looked down at the molten stone. "And from this lava, the ground we stand on was formed and continues to be formed. Like an infant, this world is still vulnerable and weak."

Fire scoffed; to him, Mud often seemed to talk rubbish.

"But as you can see, what was young has now become this mighty world which can give and provide so much," Mud continued. He turned to Fire. "And you, Fire. You're still young. Let me make you strong."

Fire was unmoved. "One day, you will speak plainly, Mud," he said, his disapproval clear. "How could you make me strong? I am already stronger than you."

Mud was undeterred by Fire's retort.

"What makes a baby strong, Fire? A childhood of pain, anger, and hunger. What is needed is an early confrontation. A confrontation with the dangers and hardships of this world. When you see the struggles of this world, you become hardened and ready for it."

Fire, confused by Mud's strange words, turned to him quizzically. It was then that Mud pushed him down into the lava. Mud smiled and laughed as Fire's body sunk into the glowing molten stone.

Sand searched the new barracks that Mud had created, looking for Air and Fire. He hoped to convince them to come with him, away from Mud. He found Air alone in a garden courtyard full of flowers and a fountain. She was walking along the path when she saw him.

"I've come to take you and Fire away from him," Sand told her. "What has he told you? What is he making?" he said as he looked at Mud's new city. Air seemed surprised that Sand didn't know. "This is for you... You will be a King - and there will be a Queen," she said, hopefully - she would like to be a Queen.

Sand looked at the city with its soldiers and armaments. Then he looked up at the void fearfully. "You don't know what is in there..." he said quietly. "Problems. Each time I draw from it, my mind and this world become more clouded."
"We will make this world into cities..." Air said, repeating Mud's ideas.
"With people who lead, people who slave?" Sand said, looking at her questioningly. "People divided, treated differently - the creation of hate, making suffering?"

Then he looked away. "I can't change Mud; I don't know what to do about him." He spoke.
"But you and Fire aren't him. Come see this world," he told her, looking back at the evil city. "We can live well without these things..."

As Sand spoke, a figure appeared behind him. "Mud was right about you, Sand – you're spineless," came a familiar voice, now darker and more hostile.

Sand turned to see that Fire had appeared, but he was changed – he wore armour covered in soot, and his skin was scarred and burned, with smoke emanating from his eyes, which glowed red. "What happened to you?" Sand asked him, stunned.
Fire circled him like a hunting lion. "I've seen," he said, glancing at the void. "If you do nothing, you'll destroy us!"
Fire, his mind infected with Mud's paranoia, had looked into the void and saw a black army forming.

Sand took Air's hand. "Don't go with him," Fire growled.
Sand released Air's hand and walked towards Fire, trying to reason with him.
"Fire, I don't know what Mud told you..." he began, but Fire interrupted him abruptly.
"I have seen the purest power and merged with it! Everyone will know me by the power's name: I am 'Hatred'!" he announced.
Sand realised that things were changing in ways he could no longer understand. "What are you?" he asked Hatred, truly confused.
Hatred walked towards him. "You don't matter," he spoke into Sand's face. "You're a footnote!"

Then, Mud appeared in the background, like Hatred; he now wore a new garb, a decorated suit of armour. Hatred glanced at Mud.
"Why do you think Mud looks exactly like you?" he asked Sand.
Sand looked at them both, confused. Hatred smirked at his confusion. "He is becoming you, superseding you. Your past will be erased. While I may be power, Mud is greatness...." He told Sand.
Sand started to back away as Hatred and Mud walked closer.
"He can think better than you..." Hatred told Sand. "Mud will be the first true thinker. He is the great identity of this new kingdom. And we have a name for a great identity. People will call him... 'Ego.'"
Hatred and Ego smiled at each other. Their frightening new despotic ideology now bound them.

Sand realised he could not win, here and now. He would have to flee. He looked to Air in a final hopeful gesture.
"Air, come with me...!" he called.
Ego laughed. "Why would a Queen follow a pauper?"
Air paused, confused. Hatred, seeing this, launched himself at Sand, outraged. He and Sand started to fight as the black hole of the void spun slowly above them.

As they fought, Ego walked over to Air, seeing she was overcome by confusion.

"Maybe he is right... maybe we are changing things for the worse," she said, tears streaming.

Ego was annoyed by this and grabbed her roughly.

"No, no, no!" he said. "You are wrong; you are a Queen! A Queen above the other mere peasants! That's what you want, isn't it?"

He looked at Sand, who was ducking Hatred's sword strikes.

"He lives in a shack," Ego told her. "He is a cockroach living in a hut of rotting wood."

He took her hand, planning to drag her from the scene and away from Sand – but she resisted. Ego twisted her wrist and forced her against the fountain to prevent her escape.

You need to choose! Will you be a Queen or a peasant?" Ego demanded.

"Ow, A Queen! I want to be a Queen!" Air said, trying to get free – but Ego was too strong.

"Well, if you truly want that title, fight for it! Prove that you desire it!" he yelled.

With that, Ego shoved Air's head into the fountain water, starting to drown her.

"Fight for what you desire!" He cried.

Sand struggled against Hatred. He could only keep the warrior at bay, for he had a level of energy and rage far higher than his own. They fought on the hilltop that Mud's defences had been built on. In desperation, Sand ran at the monster and tackled him, pushing him towards the edge of the hilltop, which dropped away into the jungle. Hatred roared in annoyance and threw Sand around like a ragdoll. Sand, out of options, tried to crawl away. But Hatred picked him up like a sack of potatoes and threw Sand over the hilltop's edge with a grunt. The drop was intense – and Sand feared it would kill him.

He rolled down the slope, heavily hitting the soil and occasional rock. The ground changed to ferns and bushes, which, while softer, had sharp edges of branches and twigs. He was relieved when he stopped rolling. And so, he lay bruised, broken, and unconscious on the moist soil of the jungle ground.

Ego was mad with rage. He had put Air's face in the water to teach her a lesson, but now he didn't know what he intended.

"Do you want to breathe your precious air? Prove to me that you will fight!" he screamed.

He was drunk with rage and anger, and her resistance seemed to invigorate him. Air struggled against Ego's grip, but she could not break free. She could feel the air in her lungs going wrong; she needed new air.

She screamed, and an explosion of red flame exploded over her, along with armour. Like Hatred, she had transformed under Ego's influence. Ego was thrown aside as she flew into the air and landed on the ground, panting and enraged with new energy. As her wet and matted hair moved away from her eyes, Ego noticed they were glowing red. He looked at her and smiled.

Although he said nothing, Ego was relieved that she had managed to escape his murderous grasp – he needed her as a minion, to slave for his whims. Thanks to his manipulation, Hatred and Desire would serve him.

"Good. There is a lesson here," he said as Air caught her breath.

"What makes Hatred so powerful? – his hate. Do you see? You were indecisive, passive – but desire got you what you wanted – you wanted Air and now, because you act – you get it."

He grinned at her.

"Your name is no longer Air; from here on, you will be called 'Desire'," Ego said as he walked away.

"You are a Queen now!" he declared.

She grit her teeth and grasped her sword.

" Yes. I am a Queen," she said.

Sand did not know how long he had been lying there in his broken and restless unconscious state, surrounded by the bird and animal sounds of the jungle. His body was sore, and his mind troubled, but his body had denied him the resources to move.

Meanwhile, in the hospital, it had been weeks since Ash had been in a coma. Even so, both Delvine and Leone continued to visit him. Today, on the wall, the calendar stated 23rd March.

Delvine, in the hard hospital chair, leaned back into Leone's warm body, feeling his presence. He hugged her. Ash's accident reminded them that life is short and you never know when your time has come. Meanwhile, the world continued its spin outside.

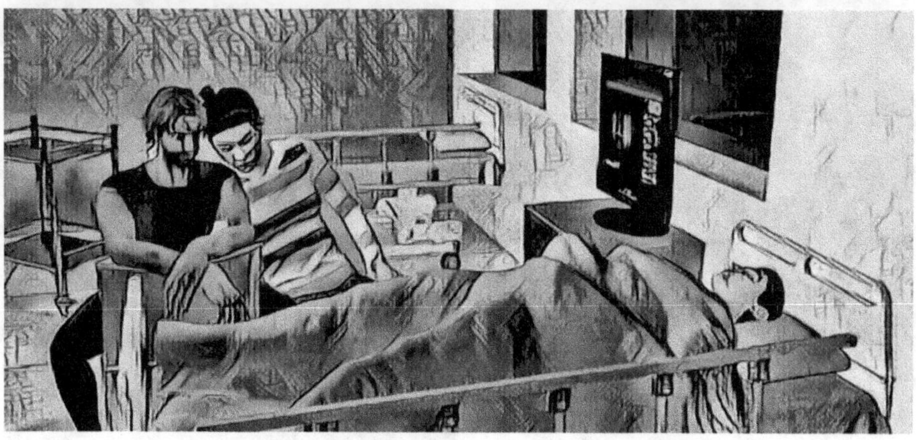

Hatred and Desire, now Ego's new and trusted generals, called their troops to fall in line. Ego, on his mount, trotted to the front. The troops began to cheer his name, beating their swords on their shields. Ego steadied his horse and spoke to them.

"My fearless army, you are the hands and arms of a new kingdom, a great empire. We are going to take this world and make it rich and powerful. All of you will share in my riches!" he called.

"My generals, the great Desire and Hatred, have made me, the new Emperor Ego, the most powerful man in this world. This world in which mere thoughts can manifest into real objects. I will make this world rewarding for all of us!"

The troops cheered in approval. Suddenly, Ego's face became serious, and he glanced at the void.

"We have enemies who would deprive us. They exist beyond the void - an army of demons!"

Ego looked back at the soldiers.

"But there is another who would leave this world in its natural, unprofitable state and leave it open to invasion from the void. His name is Sand, and he is our sworn enemy!"

He pointed to the left lines of troops.

"This battalion will go to the cave in the desert valley. There is the shrine to our enemy's vile deity, his demon adviser. You will dismantle the cave and bury the statue! The rest of you, Desire and Hatred, will accompany me down into the jungle valley. The jungle will be cleared, and we will find Sand and kill him!"

The army roared. Soon, the divisions marched as the flags of Ego flapped above them.

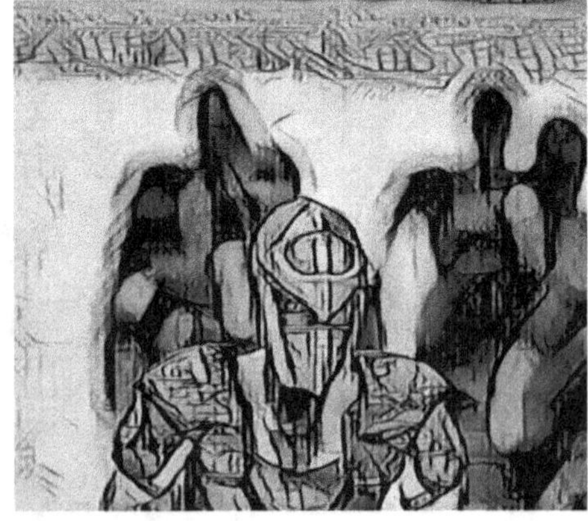

Sand lay on the ground beneath the jungle canopy, surrounded by beams of light that came and went. He wasn't sure how long he had been there. Suddenly, he heard a voice in his head.

"They are taking over, Sand! Wake up!" Nameless urged him.

Sand had never heard Nameless in his head before and was confused. Eventually, he woke up and saw a vision of Ego's soldiers at Nameless's cave, pulling down the rock mound that served as the entrance. The soldiers had almost wholly buried Nameless.

Sand woke up and sat up.

"Nameless?" he called out.

Nameless sensed Sand was awake and told him, "Sand! Once I am buried, I will no longer be able to speak to you. You are in great danger. They will cut down and burn the jungle until they find you. There is an underground tunnel in the jungle that you must find. It is your only chance to hide from Ego. The tunnel's entrance is at the far end of the Ficus Forest. Go there and follow the labyrinth. It is your only chance."

"Can't I fight him?" Sand asked, trembling with fear and pain from his fall.

"Unfortunately, when you came into this world, Sand, you carried with you negative habitual tendencies and a desire for pleasure, power, and control. Your mind has been restless as a result. Ego is the manifestation of that restlessness. We didn't have enough time to free you from this fate," Nameless explained.

"So, it's hopeless? This world is his?" Sand said, almost in tears.

The soldiers shovelled sand over Nameless, and he would soon be silenced.

"There is always hope, Sand. You must see that Ego rules your mind; on some level, you believe what he believes, fear what he fears, and want what he wants. When your mind is restless, Ego is strong. He takes over because you think you have no control over him." Nameless told Sand.

"But he has an army, I can't win." Sand said.

"Yes, he seems unbeatable. But when you see that desire, hatred, power, and ideas of immortality have no place, you'll see that Ego has no substance."

"Why didn't you tell me this before?" Sand said.

"When a man sees the bad as good and the good as bad, you can't just tell him."

They both saw that the final shovels of sand were about to cover Nameless.

"I'm sorry, Sand. But we did have some time. This journey you are on is the journey of the ages. Seek the wisdom of the past; when a man is ready, the path to freedom will reveal itself."

The sand landed, and the last edge of Nameless was covered, and he fell silent.

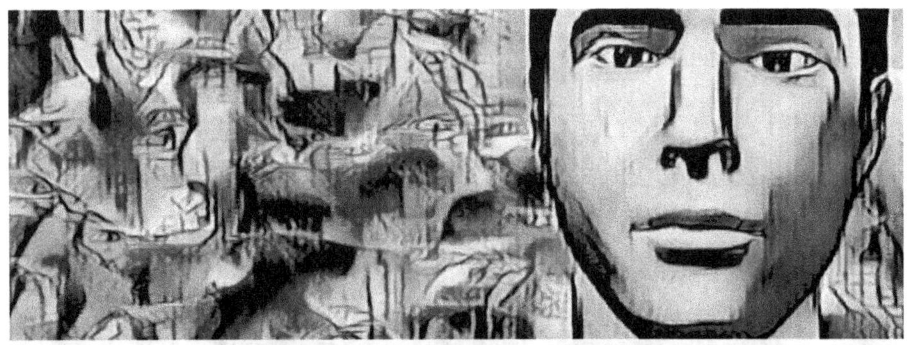

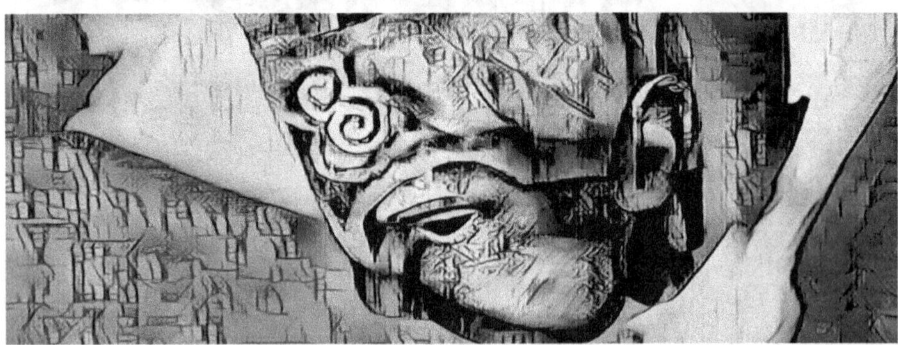

Ego, Hatred, and Desire trotted across the destroyed jungle on horseback. The great trees lay in piles, and the old stumps covered the now-open land. The soldiers had cut down or burned the trees and bushes and slashed the grass. They were capturing the fleeing animals and imprisoning them in cages made of tree branches. Emperor Ego laughed.
"You see, Desire, my Queen? He's just like a rat hiding in the undergrowth. But we have the valley surrounded. He won't escape."

Sand could hear the army's yells and the sounds of falling trees behind him as he struggled through the jungle. He knew the Ficus Forest was beyond the Bamboo Grove, as he had glimpsed it on his long rides with Mist. However, his body was bruised and cut. He stopped to wash his wounds in a stream and ripped off a strip of his shirt to tie around his bruised shoulder, hoping the compression would soothe the pain. After a strenuous climb through the swampy mud of the Bamboo Grove, he reached the flat, shady land under the Ficus Forest. It was an eerie reminder of his dream, with the vision of himself as a pig, cockerel, and snake.

Soon, he found the mysterious cave entrance and walked inside the darkness. Blinded by the dark, he walked along a tunnel deep underground. The tunnel seemed to go on and on.

Emperor Ego grew impatient. Hunting down and killing Sand would be satisfying, but he had far more to do.

He was planning to build grand buildings, cities, and places of grandiosity. He would bring others from the void to cook, clean, and toil for him. He would make them appreciate his looks, talents, and great mind. He would teach them who and what to worship, what rules to follow, who to love when to wake and sleep, and what to believe.

He was lost in these daydreams when a foot soldier approached.
"Emperor, Commander Hatred, and Desire! We have discovered an entrance to a tunnel, my lord. The traitor must have gone in there. The jungle has been cut around the valley, so there is nowhere else he could go." the foot soldier declared.
Emperor Ego grinned.
"Bring us there," he replied.

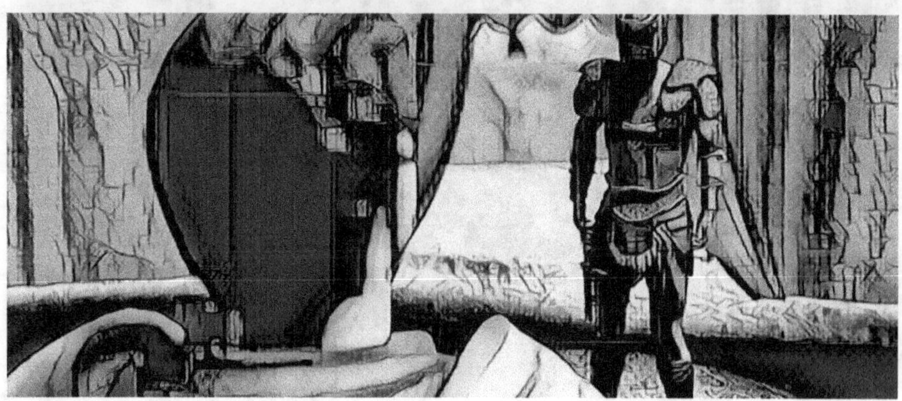

Sand eventually found that the tunnel led to a large, cathedral-like cata-comb dimly lit by mysterious candles and burning fires. The main area was filled with statues and ornaments on plinths, a large stone temple, and, just as in his dream, a large wooden table and stone relief of a cockerel, snake, and pig.

It was a strange place, seemingly empty and smelling of sandalwood and incense. Sand sat at the great table, eager to rest his weary body, and glanced around at the statues. He saw the familiar sight of an old philosopher and a Warriorress dressed in armour. But before long, he fell against the table in exhaustion.

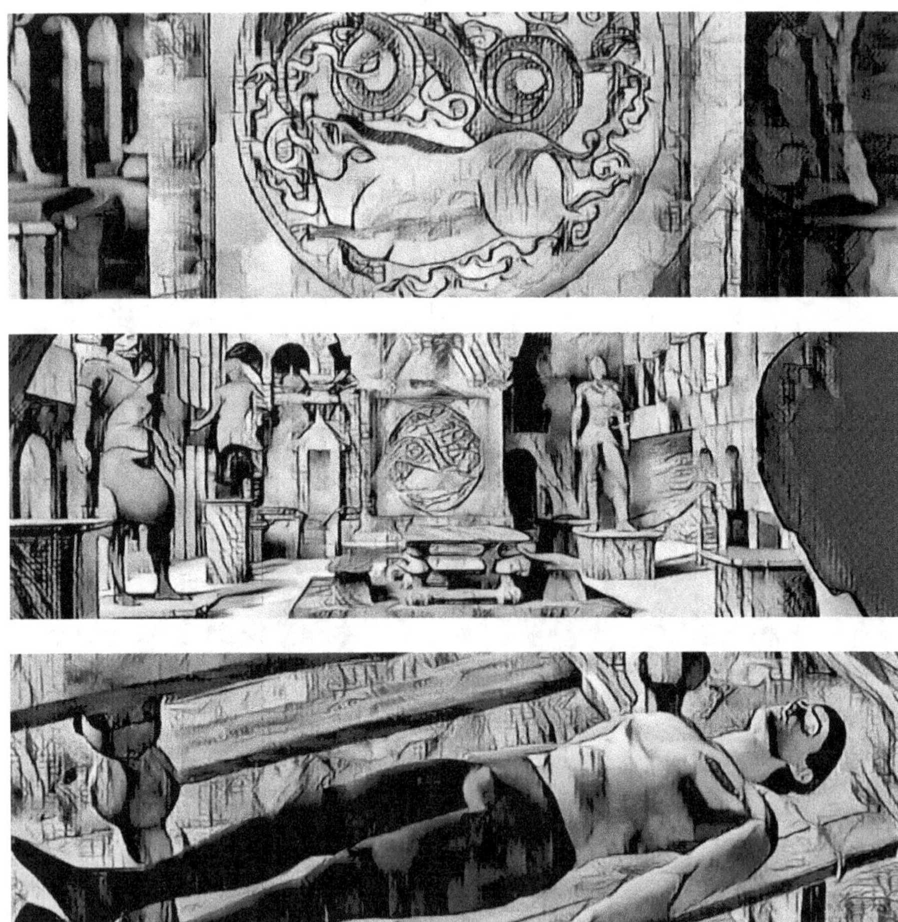

"So, this is the hole of the rat," Emperor Ego mused as he and Hatred and Desire looked at the tunnel entrance.

"Who built these places, the shrine of the demon Nameless, this tunnel?" asked Hatred.

"Who knows," Emperor Ego sneered. "Primitives, no doubt."

He bared his teeth as he spoke to Desire and Hatred.

"There are three of us and one of him. Leave the army here and take a few soldiers. This tunnel is too small for more."

Sand was startled from his fatigued slumber by a voice. "Welcome, tired traveller," it said. Sand looked up to see that the statue of the old man was moving.

"Who are you?" he asked as the statue looked down at him. The statue chuckled to himself and said:

"But a memory, a long-gone King. This labyrinth is a place of the past, of all that came before, a collection of shared human knowledge. These recollections go back to before people were people. Kingdoms, civilisations, tribes, families, armies, all here, sitting in this realm."

"Why?" Sand asked.

"There are some ideas, some things that are never lost to men," the statue said. "But it is lost; it is buried underground."

"If it is here, how do people know it?" Sand replied.

The King laughed. "How does a bird know to sit on its egg, to be a mother? That knowledge just is. We, the knowledge that there were kings, warriors, jokers, heroes, and villains, all sit here, some known and unknown. The stories of people like you and I are older than the stars."

"Then perhaps that is my destiny. I will die down here, too," he spoke.

"Perhaps. I know that evil is on your trail. But you are still alive, boy, and I know here... is not where you belong. You are no archetype. You are alive with the energy of a traveller," the King replied.

Sand was confused but remembered what Nameless had advised about listening for help. "Do you know those things that chase me?" he asked the King.

"Yes. They are immortal, as old as the first people. You are not the first, and will not be the last, to fight them," he spoke. He gestured at the rock artwork of the pig, cockerel, and snake.

"This is them?" Sand exclaimed, surprised.

"They take so many forms, but yes – this is how they can be thought of," the King replied. He gestured towards the pig. "I recognise Ego, his ignorance, pig-headedness. He thinks there is only power, pleasure, and ownership that bring meaning to life," he said.

He pointed at the cockerel. "Desire is never happy; whatever is seen, eaten, felt, or tasted is never enough. Like the chicken, she will eat and scratch at the ground, even with a full belly, and when the soil is bare," he said.

Finally, he pointed at the snake. "Hatred is never happy until the world is torn apart. He bites and spits at all things in the world," the King explained.

Sand studied the artwork for a while, mulling over both the King's and Nameless's words. He now understood that he had wanted more, hated the destructor, and misunderstood life's journey. Now, all three had poisoned him and taken control of his life.

"Then I can't win?" he asked the King.

"You cannot kill them if that's what you're asking. But you can transform, balance them," the King replied.

"Transformation? Like magic?" Sand asked.

"No. But when you see clearly, magic happens," the King explained. "All things from the void, be they the horrors or gifts, are time-limited. The destructor will take everything."

Sand thought about this, but he was unsure if it helped him.

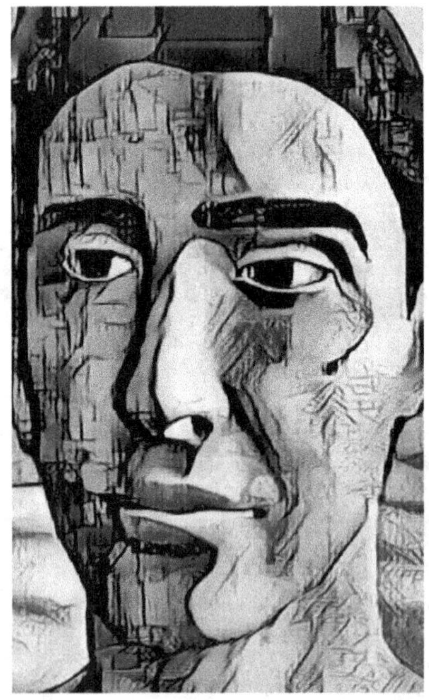

"Your sense of self, this ego person, your desire for more, hatred, came from your mind. When thoughts are to be ended is up to you, Sand," the King said.

Sand stirred uncomfortably; it all seemed too abstract and confusing.

"Up to me?" he asked. "I just wish them gone?"

"It is not about wishing them gone but understanding them completely," the King replied.

"You're saying I brought them here?" Sand said, unbelieving.

"In a way, but they are always around the corner, ready to sneak in," the King said.

"They are trying to kill me!" Sand yelled.

There was a moment of quiet from the King.

"If Ego wins, Sand, you become him. And you suffer his fate too," the King said.

Sand stood and walked away, trying to process the information.

"Ego comes about when you get caught in the snare. You are powerful, Sand, but also weak. You are made of primitive forces – hunger, pettiness, hatred – even now, you act like the destructor will not eat you up, too," the King said.

Sand sighed. "I know I'll die one day," he said, "but the rest of it doesn't make sense to me."

"You must wake up," the King said. "Do you see how Ego came to be?"

"Yes, I do," Sand sighed.

"Good. Now, break the spell you have woven. You are the most powerful one here. You can control the void up there if you want to. It's all about what you think. You ran down here to escape, but you must confront the monsters. They are forces of chaos, blind and dull. You have reason. You'll need to be smarter than them."

Sand began to weep. "I'm doomed," he cried.

"Be gentle, old man!" a female voice said. The second statue, the Warriorress, stepped down from her pedestal.

"Once, this old man was Marcus Aurelius, who led the Romans," the warrior said, looking at the King. "Another time, he was a magician or philosopher, manifested as the sage called Socrates. He represents wisdom and fairness. I am the Warriorress. Whilst his advice is wise, he forgets that talk must lead to action – and that – I can help with."

The King nodded.

"Ego himself doesn't exist, so if Ego is in this world, there must be an error in your thinking. If hatred and desire are here, you must see they are within you. See them clearly, and your foes will be finished," the King said. "But I truly believe that I understand, that I no longer hate, that I want this world to be simple again, that I and everything will end one day... I don't understand how Ego is getting bigger," Sand said.

"I will help the boy," the Warriorress said. "You have a lot to face. You have three toxins chasing you, and there are forces that have followed you into this realm. They all need to be confronted, and you will deal with them. With my help, we will follow the wise man's advice, but we need to consult the Goddess too. She will help you."

The King added more advice. "The three are cowards. They'll want to hide together. When they're separated, you'll be able to overcome them individually. Separate them, divide them. You'll have a better chance at success when they're confused and lost in the maze."
"I'll help you separate them," the warrior said. "But first, I'll take you to the Goddess."
"Who is that?" Sand asked.
"The Goddess can see the unseen. She helps anyone who asks," the King said.
"She'll teach us, Sand," the warrior said.

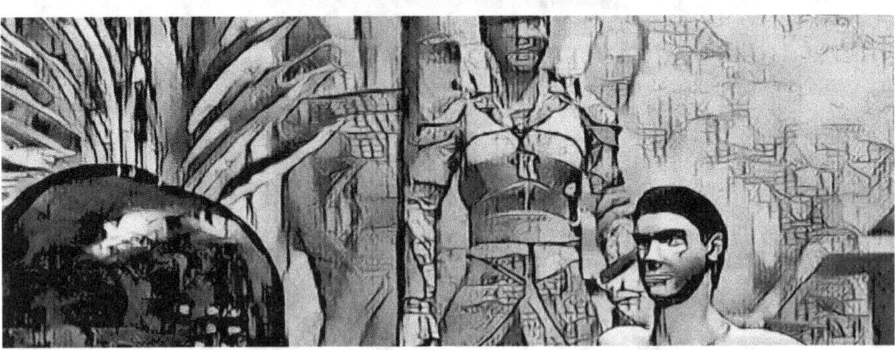

Sand and the warrioress travelled through the labyrinth, taking so many turns and doorways that Sand couldn't remember the way back. Eventually, the warrioress led him into a cave-like room as large as the one at the labyrinth's entrance. This room was star-shaped and seemed to extend upwards into what looked like a night sky or a dark cave full of glowworms. The space above twinkled and appeared vast and distant. In the centre of the room was a stone stage shaped like a lotus, with a stone frieze above it depicting the Goddess.

"We won't be disturbed here, Sand," the warrioress said. "This is the room of the healers. The healers recognise the great cosmic heart, which they see as a Goddess who embodies forgiveness, compassion, and understanding."
"Great Goddess, please come forth from the great space and manifest here," the warrioress implored the empty room. "Please come and help this worthy traveller, Sand."

"If you are pure of intention, she will come." the warrioress said as she closed her eyes and folded her hands in prayer. Sand sat down and took a deep breath, trying to let go of the spinning of his thoughts.

# ACT III

# 'THE
RISE OF THE
AUTHENTIC
SELF'

Suddenly, the room was filled with a brilliant light. From within the light, the Goddess emerged, her flowing hair and peaceful countenance a testament to her loving and supernatural nature. She floated above those who had called her.

The Goddess looked at Sand, and as she did, he could feel she saw beyond his appearance. She saw his past, his energies, the weight of his being. Soon, she had made her appraisal; she had seen him in his entirety. She was going to show him what she had seen.

"Sand," she said. "Sit and calm yourself. Breathe deeply and imagine your mind-expanding. Let go of your questions and your thoughts. Breathe out any stress, hate, or tension. Open your mind."
Sand closed his eyes and relaxed a little, feeling safe in the cave with the love he sensed from the Goddess and the protection of the Warrior-ress. He could release his worry and anxieties about Ego, Nameless, and everything at that moment.

After a moment of quiet and calm, she said, "See what you have been blind to, Sand."

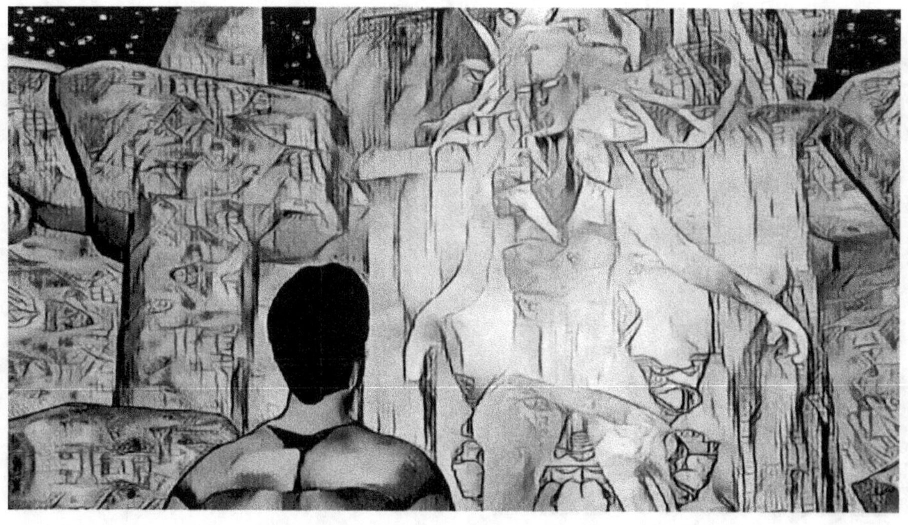

At first, Sand's mind was empty, but then a spark in his mind happened, and he felt anger and a tightness come over him. It was a feeling of wanting and being stuck. And then, in a flash, he saw Desire and Hatred, but in another time and place. They were dressed differently and had different names; Desire was Delvine, Hatred was Leone, and Sand was now called Ash.

"I see them," he said. "I knew them before." He announced.

Now Sand saw that, as Ash, he was driven by the belief that he and his pleasure were the most important. But rather than making him happy, he was angry and addicted to various pursuits. He saw past exchanges between him and Delvine and Leone. They had been friends since they were young and had grown close, but gradually that had changed. Ash had become self-obsessed and had repeatedly betrayed and deceived his friends.

"Desire and Hatred – they were friends. I rushed through my life - rushing through my life, tight and stressed. I was misguided, selfish, and dishonest," he said sadly. "They were good people, and I used that to my advantage."
Other painful visions came, him selling dangerous pills and substances to vulnerable people, leading them to all manner of pain and suffering, other deceits, betrayals and harms done to himself and others. Sand was mortified.
"I sold people dangerous pills - to vulnerable people, leading them to pain and suffering; so much harm was done to myself and others."

Then, a new vision came to him. He was unconscious, lying helpless in a bed, and despite his wrongdoings, his friends were sitting at his bedside, wishing for his well-being and recovery. In a wave of pain and sorrow, Sand saw his karma. He longed to release his hatred, desire, and delusion.

"Do you see, Sand?" the Goddess said. "You did not come here empty." The goddess knew that Sand had bad karma, that he had taken advantage of two friends and mistreated them. Sand's nemeses, "Desire" and "Hatred", were the reenactment of his unfinished relationship with them.

"Now that you see your past mistakes, you must let go of them. You should not repeat them and put your effort into changing your actions and thoughts. When you do, you become blameless, free of pain or guilt or any more wanting, hatred, or sadness." she explained.

More than anything, Sand wanted to be free. 'How do I let go?' he asked her.

The King stood alone at the entrance to the Labyrinth, waiting for the arrival of the Three Toxins. He knew they would come for Sand. The King, a long-time inhabitant of the Labyrinth, understood that his realm was built of pure consciousness, where all archetypes existed. He was the archetype of hard work, fairness, and governance. He knew he had a duty to protect anyone from evil, particularly Ego, the manifestation of self-centeredness.

Ego would kill Sand and take control of Sand's realm. The King understood this was a battle for Sand's mind. As he waited, The King formulated a plan. He knew the Three Toxins were cowards. If he could separate them, Sand might stand a chance.

Ego arrived first, holding his sword and looking determined to find his prey. He was followed closely by Hatred and Desire. The King watched calmly as they approached.
"Welcome, Toxins," The King said. "I have been expecting you."
Ego sneered at The King, puffing himself up as he stepped towards the monarch. "Move aside, old statue. We are here in the sewers to find Sand; there is nothing you can do to stop us," he declared.

The King narrowed his eyes, standing his ground. "I will not let you harm him or anyone. You are not welcome here."
Ego laughed. "And who are you to stop us? You are down here in this forgotten subconscious void while I have manifested in the conscious realm. You are no match for us."

The King was not bothered by Ego's arrogance. "I may be just an idea, but I am a great and powerful one – the archetype of hard work, fairness, and governance. I must protect those in need, and I will not stand by and let you hurt Sand. You may think you are powerful, but you are nothing but a coward," he said. "You hide behind your wants, letting them dictate your every move. You are nothing but a puppet, controlled by your delusion of self-importance."

Ego roared in anger. "How dare you speak to me like that," he yelled. "I am the embodiment of the greatest force in the universe; I am Man's ambitions made real. You are nothing but a weak, old fool!"
The King shook his head, his expression sad. "You are not powerful, Ego. You are a slave, and it will be your downfall. You are not in control of your actions, making you weak. It is time to face the truth before it consumes you completely."

Ego was livid, his anger reaching a boiling point. "I will never change – I am strength and power. It is who I am."

The King sighed, his eyes full of sorrow. "Then you will never truly be free, Ego. You will be nothing but a pawn in an arbitrary game. You exist in a never-ending cycle of foolishness, and it will be your undoing."

Ego growled and moved towards the King, sword ready. He ordered Hatred and Desire away.

"Find Sand and kill him. I will stay and kill the King; I think I will enjoy it!" Ego said.

Hatred and Desire followed his command and exited through one of the tunnels.

The King knew Ego was not one to back down, and he prepared himself for the fight that was to come. He would give Sand the time he needed.

'How do you let go, Sand? You have started to see the truth by emptying your mind. You have seen that the world is made of strings, and you have all the hooks. Straighten your hooks, and you'll never be caught up again." The Goddess said, answering Sand's question. "But there is more, Sand. Close your eyes."
Sand did so. Next, Sand found himself levitating into the cave, along with the Goddess, up to the dark space above, in the glimmer of the lights.

"Be appreciative and grateful. See all that is good. The blue skies and the sun make the plants grow. This world holds you, supports you, feeds you, the water that nourishes you... Without asking, love surrounds you. It gives freely with each breath you take. You inhale the love that this cosmos is formed of." The Goddess spoke.
As Sand fell deeper into peace, tranquillity, and relaxation.
"This is your mind, Sand when you hold onto nothing—no armies, war, questions, thoughts - just peace. Here, you, I, and all things are one." the Goddess said as her light flooded over him.
"The great unity that holds you loves you. It can heal you; it can heal anything. It will be here when all is done when all is said."

Sand looked at his hands; they were glowing with her light.

"You are a dance of energy, of things coming and going. Remember yourself as more than a material man with material concerns; letting go, forgiveness, and resolution will be easy. When you calm and subdue the mind, you become and reconnect with a great stream of energy and consciousness that is this great unity." She spoke, and Sand understood that his material life was only a passing moment; he was part of a greater whole.

Sand and the Goddess slowly fell back to the room floor as the meditation ended. Sand knew he had to reverse his errors. It would not be easy, but he felt a sense of hope and determination.

"What cannot be transformed, managed, or killed will be conquered by love?" said the Goddess as she disappeared back into the stone frieze. If he could transform his mind, then his demons would be defeated.

The Warriorress brought Sand to the labyrinth's armoury. "Take this armour and this sword," she told Sand. She could sense his uncertainty. "Yes, you do not wish to do so," the Warrioress continued, "But I'm afraid that sometimes we may need to. But you can have a sword and not use it." Her words lingered in the air, a poignant reminder of the necessity of action in life.

The Warrioress knew Sand's reluctance - but action and preparedness were necessary in a world plagued by chaos.
"For now, see it as a symbol of your strength," she implored, her voice softer, layered with empathy. "Your willingness to stand up to chaos and be unshakable in the face of horror; perhaps you will never have to brandish it." She said reassuringly.
There was a weightiness to her words. The sword she offered was not just a weapon but a manifestation of resolve, a token of readiness in a world fraught with uncertainty. The Warrioress hoped it would remain sheathed, a symbol of strength untarnished by the horrors it might unleash.

Sand and the Warrioress observed from their concealed vantage point as Hatred and Desire strolled along the labyrinthine path ahead.

"This place is supposed to be filled with the great ideas of humankind – Ha! So why is it like an endless maze of dusty rubbish?" Desire exclaimed with disdain.

"This place is strange, unusual. Sand, come out! Perhaps the emperor will have mercy on you," Hatred bellowed, his voice carrying echoes of malice.

"We have to trick them into splitting up," Sand whispered urgently to the Warrioress. "If we can separate them, I might stand a chance. I will lead Hatred away."

The Warrioress nodded, a fierce determination gleaming in her eyes.

"I will take care of Desire," she declared, embodying bravery and action, unflinching in the face of either Hatred or Desire.

Sand stepped forward, emerging from their hiding spot, fixing his gaze on Hatred.

"I challenge you to a one-on-one fight," he proclaimed, his voice steady and unwavering.

Hatred, catching sight of Sand, sneered in contempt, his anger a blazing inferno.

"You are no match for me," he spat, his tone seething with arrogance.

But Sand remained undaunted. He knew that to defeat Hatred, he must stay calm and focused, resisting the fiery soldier's attempts to incite anger.

The Warrioress walked out to back up Sand, and Desire yelled: "Look out! It's an archetype from the maze. Back away, Beast! Sand is ours!"

In the labyrinth's heart, amidst the tense standoff between Hatred and Sand, the Warrioress diverted her focus to Desire. The embodiment of craving, lust, and insatiable want, Desire exuded formidable energy, yet the Warrioress remained resolute, undeterred by the looming challenge. She walked up to Desire.

"You don't have to do this," the Warrioress spoke softly, her voice carrying a plea. "You can choose a different path. You don't have to be controlled by your desire."

"Soon, I will be crowned the Queen of the Kingdom of Cognito. I am not controlled by anything - I control! And what are you?" Desire countered, her voice dripping with defiance.

"I am the Warrioress," the response echoed with quiet strength.

"A fighter? Why do you protect this worm? He wants no power," Desire taunted, attempting to provoke a reaction.

"A true warrior can fight well and possesses the strength to kill, but true strength lies not in combat. It's in finding ways to avoid it. To control emotions and seek peace defines a great warrior, one with power yet chooses not to wield it," the Warrioress explained, her words a testament to her principles.

"Now I understand why you defend him. You are also weak!" Desire retorted, preparing her weapon, determined to bring down the Warrioress. Recognising that mere words wouldn't sway Desire, the Warrioress readied herself, understanding the imminent clash that words alone couldn't prevent.

As the two women engaged in battle, Sand seized the opportunity, slipping away from the grip of Hatred into the labyrinth's shadows. Hatred, infuriated, cursed and gave chase, leaving Desire alone to confront the Warrioress in a fierce battle of wills and strength.

Sand ran with Hatred close behind him for a while, but he led him into the spiral room, filled with staircases, passages, and windows to confuse Hatred.

"I'm ready for you," Sand said from another room.

Hatred looked for a way to find Sand.

"You bastard! Come closer!" Hatred yelled, his face twisted with anger and malice. The flames around his head burned brighter.

"Why do you want to kill me, Hatred?" Sand asked, his voice shaking slightly.

"Because you are weak, Sand," Hatred replied, his voice cold and cruel; he continued to run, seeking Sand, his heavy armour gradually exhausting him.

Now that Hatred was slower, Sand appeared in front of him.

"But I know why you appeared here, Hatred. When I allowed anger and hatred to consume me, it created you. And now you want to kill me, and you suffer too." Sand told him.

"You're talking rubbish!" Hatred hissed. "How do I suffer?"

Sand hung his head. "I led you down this dark path, along with Ego."

"Do you remember when you first came from the void? You were content and calm. But now you wake up tight and full of anger and sleep in anger. That is a life of suffering. Whether your enemies live or die, you burn."

"Burn?" Hatred questioned, looking at himself. Amid chaos and conflict, Hatred hadn't noticed that he was engulfed in flames, manifesting his burning fury and torment.

"I can release you from your flames," Sand offered, stepping closer, his voice calming. Hatred, amidst his suffering, looked upon Sand, recognising the anguish within his rage and fiery intensity.

"But who will save your world?" Hatred questioned, torn between his turmoil and the greater purpose.

"I'll do it, Hatred. I'm going to make this place right. You don't have to fight for me or it," Sand assured, extending an olive branch of understanding and resolution. Overwhelmed, Hatred collapsed to his knees, tears streaming down his face, an emotional release of agony and despair.

"I need you to see why you're here." Sand told Hatred, hoping to free him.

"Please. I don't want to exist like this," Hatred said with sadness.

With eyes closed in concentration, Sand conjured a vision in their midst. A hospital room materialised, depicting Sand in a weakened state, surrounded by familiar faces—Leone and Delvine seated vigilantly beside him.

"In my meditation, I saw that you are an old friend, Fire. You gave me good advice, had my back, and only wanted the best for me," Sand reflected, recounting his revelations. "I let myself down, I let you down, and dragged you into my realm."

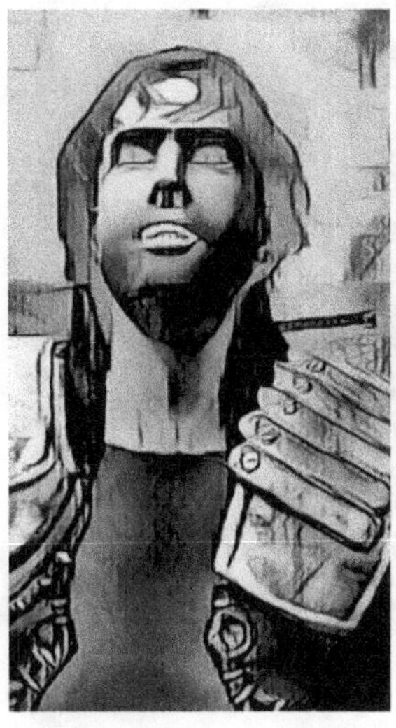

Hatred's armour faded, and the flames around his head cooled and stopped. He looked at Sand, wide-eyed. "You're right. This isn't me. Ego lied about everything," he said. Hatred's armour faded, and the flames around his head cooled and stopped. He faded into his real-world form – Leone. He looked at Sand wide-eyed, and his sword fell to the ground.
"I will do everything possible to make amends for my past actions. Please, Fire, let me move on," Sand said, looking up at him.

Leone laughed. "I know where I'm meant to be, Sand. I'm going home," he said. He stood up.
"Learn from your mistakes, make things right, and go in peace, Sand," he said, turning and walking away before disappearing completely.

Sand sighed in relief, feeling as though a great weight had been lifted off his shoulders. He knew he still had a long road ahead of him. "We'll meet again, Fire," Sand said, knowing that he would see Leone again, somehow.

The clash between Desire and the warrior raged with intensity and determination. Desire, fuelled by a craving for supremacy as the realm's Queen, possessed a swiftness and guile that made her a formidable adversary. The Warriorress, skilled and courageous, struggled against Desire's toxic influence, though her resolve remained unyielding.

Desire's strikes with her sword proved futile against the warrior's stone-like body. Effortlessly, the Warriorress tossed Desire to the ground, yet the power-hungry woman swiftly rebounded, thrusting the Warrioress against a stone wall, causing rocks to cascade upon her. Undeterred, the Warrioress emerged from the debris, seizing Desire in a chokehold and forcibly casting her aside.
"Leave the labyrinth, Desire, and your troubles will cease," the Warrioress urged.
"Never!" Desire vehemently retorted.

Seizing a nearby relic, Desire hurled it toward the Warriorress. Caught off guard, the Warriorress lost her footing, tumbling from the walkway into the catacombs below. She lay still amidst the shadows. Triumphant, Desire stood at the pit's edge, a smug satisfaction adorning her features. She vanished into the labyrinth with a self-satisfied smile, leaving the fallen female warrior behind.

Desire entered the junction of tunnels and found Sand waiting.
"Where's Hatred gone?" she asked him.
"He's found a new fight, I guess." Sand replied.
"No matter." She laughed, not believing him. She raised her fists. "Stand and fight, Sand."

"In my past lives, I have been driven by wanting and craving," he said. "When you want too much, it becomes a force inside you, like a cancer, and it can follow you across realms. It's called karma."

"Talk, talk, talk, Sand," she spoke. "I do not care. You stand in our way, in my way, in the way of all my kingdom's desires!"

"I was like you; I wanted things from the void. But I see now that it could not give me what I needed. But through my spiritual guide, Nameless, and the Goddess, I have understood that desire only leads to suffering. There's nothing that a person could receive that will bring more than temporary happiness because people always long for more. The things we want are subject to change, and the more you have, the more you worry about losing it." Sand implored.

"That's fine, but I'm not like you. I will forever be happy as a Queen of Ego's Realm." Desire countered.

But Ego's world will not be what you want, right?" Sand asked her. " Desire. Tell me truthfully: What kind do you want?"

Desire's face turned white - she had never thought about it before. Sand saw his chance.

"I've seen you in the previous realm, Desire. I know why you appeared to me in that pool. You and Fire were good, content, happy and real people." Desire's eyes widened as Sand's words reminded her of something forgotten.
"I did this to you, Desire. It was my desires that affected you. I have infected you with my wants, but as I let go, I know you will be freed, too," Sand said.

Desire stumbled backwards as if she had been pushed; she was seeing things she had not before.
Sand steadied his voice despite his racing heart.
"I see now that my bad actions created you, and I am deeply sorry for wronging you. I took my only true friends and turned them against me."
Desire faltered for a moment; she couldn't move as Sand spoke.
"Do you remember your true self? Sand continued, his voice softening.

As Sand spoke, Desire's power and anger seemed to dissipate. Tears streamed down her face as she listened to Sand's words, and finally, she changed back into Delvine. " Yes, I remember, Sand.
I forgive you. I'm waiting for your return to us." she said, her voice barely above a whisper. She smiled at him, and then, just like that, she vanished.

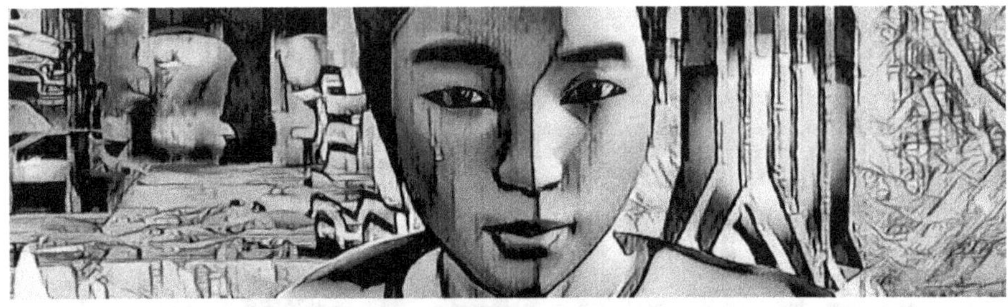

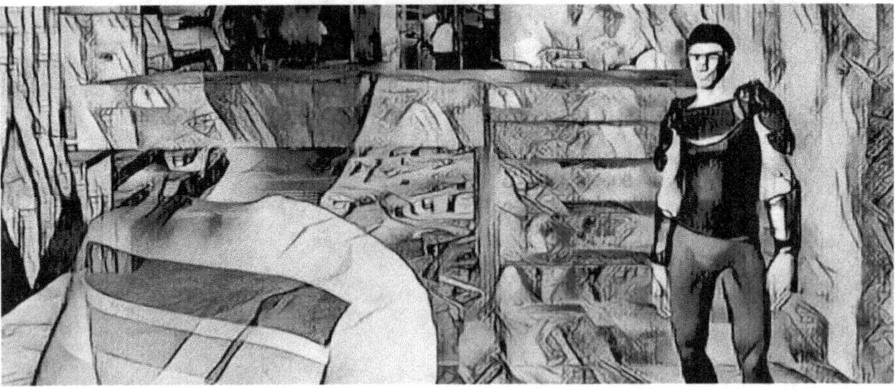

The battle was fierce and intense, Ego hacking with his sword, but the King was surprisingly lithe. "You overestimate your abilities, Ego! Watch!" The King's words preceded a swift kick that swept Ego off his feet. Ego fled into the shadows, seeking refuge atop a nearby ruin, hatching a new plan. "Come out, Ego. Leave this place or face me. Why does the great ego hide? Bring yourself before me so I may remedy you!" the King called out.

From a chandelier, Ego swung, sending a heavy frieze crashing down upon the King, shattering his form. Ego looked down at the shattered statue.

"Tell me, old man, how many times have I, the Ego, risen victorious over a King? I may be a product of Sand's mind, but I even know how many Kings become despots, serving the likes of me. You could have shared in my new kingdom," Ego taunted. "Far too often, men have followed your evil kind in countless times and realms," the King retorted. "And therefore, those of true and honest character forever must fight back."

Ego straightened his uniform, wiping blood from his face. "Till we meet again, now, I have a world to claim," he declared before turning and vanishing back into the Labyrinth, leaving the King to face his demise alone in the entrance room.

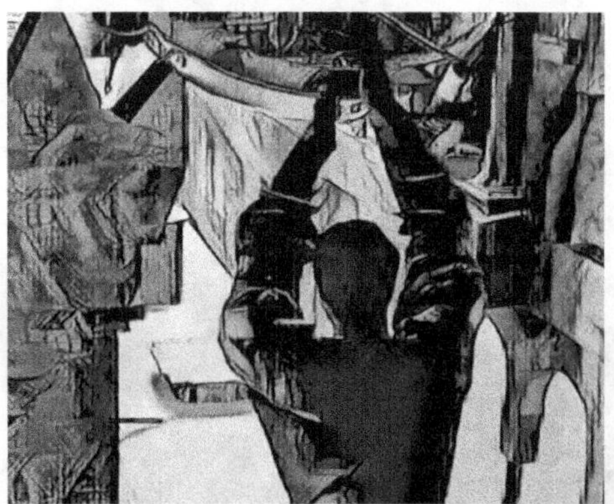

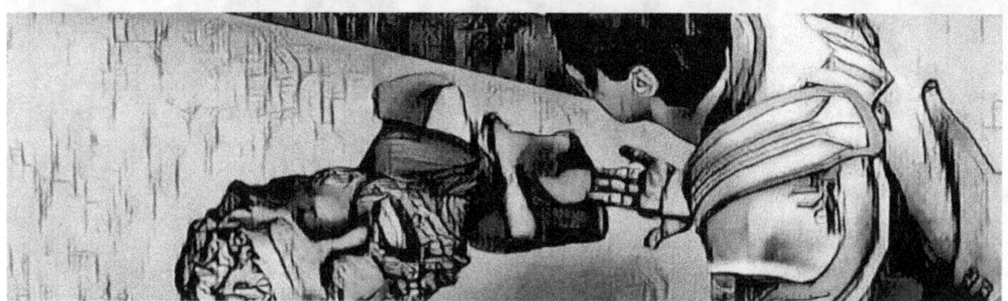

Within the labyrinth's twisting tunnels, Ego pressed forward; suddenly, he heard Sand's voice reverberating through his mind:
"Ego. Ego. Can you hear me?" Sand's words seemed to permeate the very air. "I'm here. Keep walking. Ego. You'll be with me soon."
Turning a corner, Ego stepped into a chamber —a place Sand had chosen for the impending confrontation.

"At last." Ego's voice rang out, laced with determination and hostility. "Have you finally decided to face me? Now, you will die, and we will be bound together. Don't worry. It will only be a small death," Ego declared.
Sand stood firm, unwavering in the face of Ego's antagonism. His eyes, pools of resolve, locked onto Ego's.
"I've finally realised the truth," Sand began, his voice carrying a weight of self-discovery. "You are a manifestation of my false beliefs in power, status, and wealth. I've been thinking about you, Ego. How did you go from having no power to having it all?"
Sand's voice carried both accusation and revelation. " Once, you didn't exist - and now I fight you daily! But I know why - this place was still, quiet, and serene. But I wanted more. I asked for treasures and pleasures and wanted them to last forever! I took from the void, I argued with death, I raged at this world, and then I started to think I could rule it all."

Ego scoffed, his disdain palpable. "You are nothing but a mortal. You think you can understand me.? Ha! I am necessary. You can't live without me. You haven't a clue. Do you think you would have anything without me? You'd be in the dark ages. What kind of future do you have without money? Big walls and people caring for you. See, you are no match for me and my wondrous mind." Ego proclaimed, dismissing Sand's understanding.

Sand, filled with a mixture of disdain and determination, confronted the very essence of Ego. "And here you are, a selfish, self-centred, manipulating coward. You want it all: my memories, my thoughts; you want to kill me and take over. And I've been letting you!"

"Hah! But you are nothing but a weakling. You will never defeat me." Ego snapped, dripping with arrogance.
Yet Sand stood resolute. "Remember the first time you appeared?" His words cut through the tension, carrying the weight of revelation. "I sat down, I meditated, and then you were gone. Why was that? What are you, Ego? Thanks to some good advice, I've worked it out. You see, this place has all the great shared ideas of humankind. And this place - is the 'Seat of Pure Mental Awareness."
Ego sneered at the circular space adorned with ancient keystones and a golden stand displaying a giant crystalline orb.

"Hah! This place will be forgotten. And I will return to Cognito to rule."
He voiced.

Then, pointing at the orb displaying swirling images of Ego, Sand, Hatred, and Desire, Sand emphasised his revelation. " Look for yourself. Here it all is. The thoughts, the sights, smells, memories…"

Ego acknowledged the display, " Yes. It's beautiful!" he conceded.

"Yes. You should like it. It's what you are. You see the things you cling to. Memories. Desires. Likes. Dislikes. Urges. See how they come and go?" Sand continued, steering the focus.

But Ego remained steadfast: "Indeed. But this is you, too."

"Maybe. But the day I first conquered you, I saw that I was not only the reflection on this ball but the ball itself. When I detach from these reflections and empty my awareness, you don't exist. Then there's only my authentic self - with no wants, hate, or mistaken beliefs." Sand declared, unveiling his realisation.

Ego chuckled darkly. " Hahaha. Perhaps I will keep you as a jabbering idiot for my amusement, Sand!"

Sand acted decisively. "Watch." He spoke.

With a gentle touch, Sand tipped the orb, causing light, images, and mist to dissolve. Simultaneously, Ego vanished. Serenely, Sand restored the orb, and his thoughts returned to the ball - accompanied by Ego, who screamed in agony.

"You will pay for that!" Ego roared.

But Sand remained composed. "There you go. You never have indeed existed. You're a bunch of old habits." He remarked.

"Hah! You can't hold back forever. You'll have to leave here one day." Ego scoffed. He guessed Sand couldn't hold the ball forever.

"This is the end, Ego. I have learned well now what is beneficial and what is not. I know the moral from the immoral. I have become wise. I know what to intend, do, say. Today, I renounce my old name, memories, urges, and plans for the future. And it starts now." Sand solemnly declared.

" You….!" Ego sneered. "I'm immortal. I will live forever!"

Ego started to jab at Sand, but he was fading, weak - his strikes were fruitless and passed through Sand without even moving a hair.

With closed eyes and focused intent, Sand emptied his mind. The orb went blank. Gradually, Ego weakened and groaned - crumbling to the ground, feeble and insignificant, dissipating into nothingness.

Sand slowly sat down in the temple's sanctum; Sand continued his meditation until the orb radiated with a transcendent brilliance. Ego was defeated, and tranquillity and liberation were reinstated in his world.

Sand approached the entrance to the labyrinth with a heavy heart. He had won the battle against Ego, but at a terrible cost. The smouldering torches guided sand as he made his way through the winding corridors of the labyrinth. He soon emerged into a large chamber and saw his comrade, the Warriorress. She turned to face him, and he thanked her for her courage and strength, to which she nodded in response.

"The King - Ego smashed him." She said, gesturing to the shattered statue in the chamber's centre. The king's head was placed gently back on his body.
Sand knelt and paid his respects, tears streaming down his face.
"Great King, thank you. You were a great comrade - even though our moments were so short." He said.

He had won the battle against Ego, but at a terrible cost. He could not help but feel profound grief for his comrade, the King, who had sacrificed his life in the fight.
"One day, the King may form here again if beings are wise and honourable. But it may not be for years, an age, or perhaps – if men are wicked – until the next realms come.' The Warriorress said.
'I will keep his message alive in my life.' Sand told her.
'Yes, my friend. May you journey well.' She told him.

Sand then made his way to the Room of the Healers and lit some incense at the shrine of the Goddess, offering his thanks for her wisdom and advice. Sand remembered the Goddess' words of wisdom, which had helped him see his past mistakes and the path to victory.

She had taught him to look within himself and find strength in his heart, and he was forever grateful for her guidance. He lit some incense at her shrine to thank her, knowing that without her help, he would have been lost. The Goddess had also told Sand about the power of forgiveness and how it could free him from the grip of Ego. She had reminded him to be kind to himself and to show compassion for all beings. Sand had taken these lessons to heart and was now ready to face the outside world with a new sense of peace and contentment.

Sand was stunned by the sight before him as he stepped out of the labyrinth and back into the outside world. It was as if a hundred years had passed, and the jungles had grown back. Ego's kingdom was in ruins, and Ego's army had disappeared.

Sand felt a sense of peace and hope as he looked around, knowing that the outcome he had worked so hard for had finally been achieved. He looked up to the sky, feeling the sun's warmth on his face, and knew that the King would be proud of him.

Sand returned to Nameless's shattered shrine, his heart heavy with grief for his friend and physical and mental exhaustion. As he trudged through the rubble, he was suddenly greeted by the joyful clucking of his beloved pet chicken, Peck. He hugged the bird, and with tears streaming down his face, Sand fell to his knees and began to dig frantically through the debris, searching for the statue of Nameless.

At last, he uncovered the head and shoulders of his benevolent guide, and he cried out in relief to see his old friend.

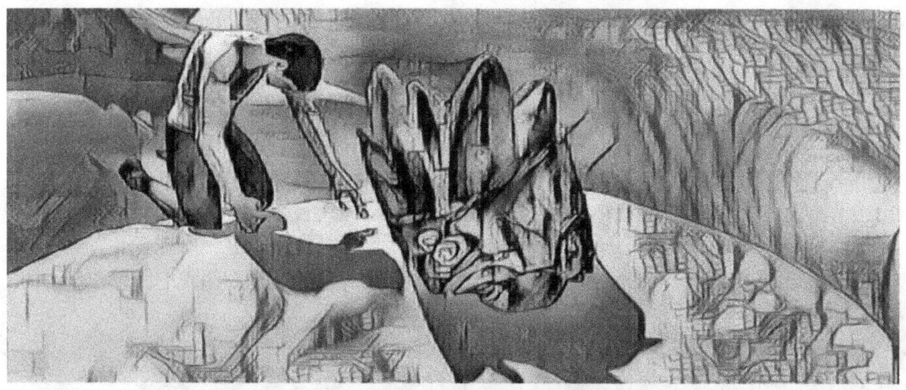

With his head revealed, Nameless spoke again, his voice gentle and comforting. "Well done, Sand," he said. "You have fought bravely and triumphed over the false beliefs of Ego. Now it is time to focus on cultivating a mind of grateful and content thoughts and keeping your desires and dislikes in check."
Sand smiled for the first time in what felt like an eternity. "I believe I can do that, Nameless," he said. "For the first time in my life, I feel like I can truly be free."
Nameless nodded, his wise eyes shining. " It is time for you to return to the kingdom of your mind and the world of materiality, the world of humans," he said. "The path back is to take the Reaper's door and leave this place."

"I can't stay here?" Sand asked.
"You return because you must. Perhaps when you learn those worldly lessons, you will manifest in other places like myself. Perhaps eventually, you will obtain a complete release from materiality and be freed, entirely extinguished from the suffering realms and brought back into the light of the divine unity." Nameless explained.
Sand nodded tears of gratitude and joy streaming down his face. He placed a wreath of flowers over Nameless's shoulders, a sign of appreciation and respect.

As he turned to leave, Nameless called out one last time. "Sand," he said, "never forget the lessons you have learned here. Keep your mind and heart pure, and you will find true happiness in this life and beyond."

Sand returned to the valley of the Destructor, knowing it was time to leave this realm and return beyond. The thought of facing the Destructor made his heart pound, but he knew this was due to his old conception of death.

The valley was thick with fog. He noticed new bones, a scent of decay, and the distant cawing of crows. The dry sand whipped around him as gusts of wind blew through the valley, giving him a sense of desolation and despair. The bones of once-living beasts saddened him as he trekked further down the path. He could feel the Reaper's presence looming closer, but still, he kept his sense that he had made the whole journey in this world for this purpose.

He had thought about his world, a world of thoughts and ideas come to life, and decided to call it 'Cognito'. He had seen the word on one of the pillars he had pulled from the void and knew it was about the mind and thinking.

Cognition made this world, and thanks to Nameless and his comrades in the labyrinth, he was here and free of Ego.

Finally, after what seemed like hours, the portal to the Reaper's lair appeared before him, up the slope of sand at the base of a rust-coloured cliff. He walked up to the ancient doorway and hesitated at the entryway. In the etchings of the pillar, amongst the myriad of text and symbols, he noticed the words "Exeuntes Cognitum". He took this as the exit from this world, the world he had named - or possibly that had been called that all along.

He looked into the darkness and took one last deep breath before entering, knowing this was it - here he would face his final greatest fear. He felt his way along the black tunnel with his fingers and finally came to a room inside. A fire was burning in that space, and the black-robed Reaper's figure sat in a great chair.

The room's darkness was suffocating, and he felt terrified that he could not see the exit. His steps were heavy with the weight of his fear.

The Reaper sensed him and turned to look at him, with only his white eyes visible. Sand's heart raced faster as the figure slowly stood. He could almost feel the Reaper's presence looming, and his natural reaction was a sense of dread, but he also felt a strange sense of familiarity.

But Sand forced himself to control his racing mind and slow his breathing. He reminded himself that this threshold was not the end but the beginning of a transformation. He let the tension in his shoulders go and let go of his fears.

The Destructor did not move; it looked at him as if questioning his presence. It did not raise a hand or try to touch him. Sand took advantage of that. He took some moments to ensure that his fear was tamed. He focused on the warmth of the flames and the cave's darkness and used the Reaper's white eyes as objects to focus on.

Finally, calm and satisfied with the why and how of his decision to face the entity, he slowly reached out and pulled the Reaper's hood away.

With a sudden realisation, Sand saw that it was him. He felt an inexplicable acceptance as he looked into his own eyes. This was his mind, and the Reaper was part of it. At that moment, he understood that all fear was conquered if he was the Reaper. He knew this was his moment of truth.

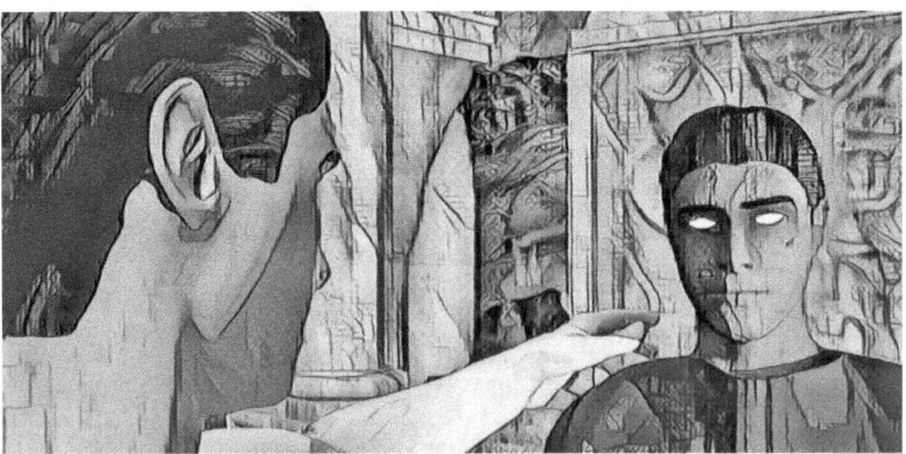

Like the buffalo and Mist before him, he saw particles coming off his skin and floating towards the Destructor. As this happened, he felt a strange transformation as he dissolved into the Reaper. Sand realised that this was not death at all but rather a rebirth.

The truth was finally revealed to him: he needed to be transformed to move forward. He was humbled by the realisation that this was one transformation of many that would lead him to a new beginning, towards ultimate freedom and peace. He accepted his destiny and was dissolved entirely, disappearing into the darkness of the void.

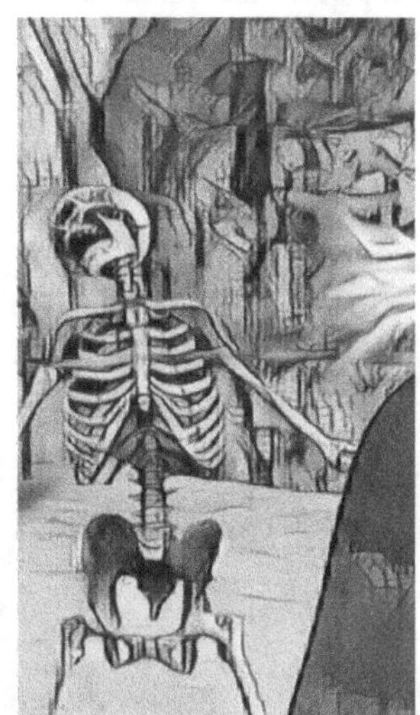

Delvine was the first to notice his movements, calling out to Leone as she rushed to the bed. "Ash! He's Awake!"
Leone, who had been gazing out the window, spun around and darted towards the bed. "What?" he exclaimed to Delvine, stunned by the possibility of Ash waking.
"Can you hear us, Ash?" he called as he reached the bed.

Sand couldn't speak, but his eyes conveyed a heartfelt apology to his friends. He knew his journey wasn't over; each day was a second chance at life, and he was determined to make the most of every moment.

Outside, the city hummed—a tapestry of brief, fleeting lives, each person living their private journey.

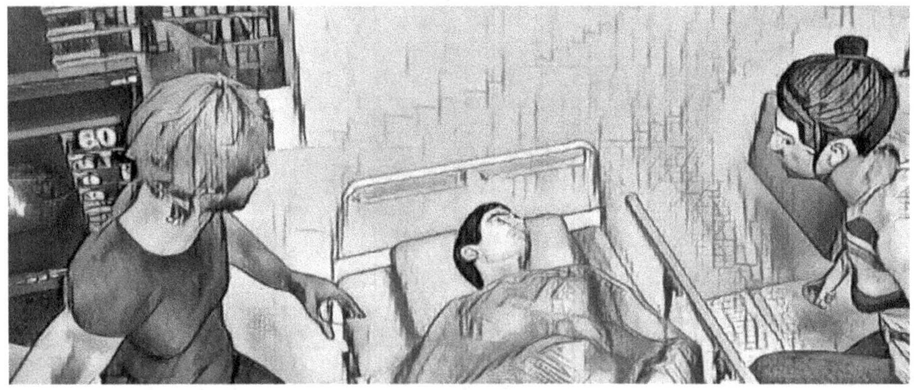

# ABOUT THE AUTHOR

**KARL-HEINZ SCHRADT** is a multi-talented creative, seamlessly blending artistry, advocacy, and mental health expertise. Karl-Heinz was born to a German father and a Chinese-Malaysian mother. His global journey has traversed New Zealand, the UK, Australia, and Indonesia.

Professionally, he's a mental health clinician and educator, lending his expertise across diverse platforms. Beyond this, Karl-Heinz co-founded an NGO supporting wildlife and local communities on the outskirts of the Sumatran Forest.

Creatively, his repertoire is diverse: authoring 'Becoming Unshakable,' a mental health resource; crafting 'The Man from the Sand,' a compelling feature animation film; and curating the numerous titles on Galah Books and videos on YouTube, TikTok, and his website. Through Galah Books, he aims to entertain, inform, and guide audiences.